The Diary of Emily Dickinson

The Diary of
Emily Dickinson

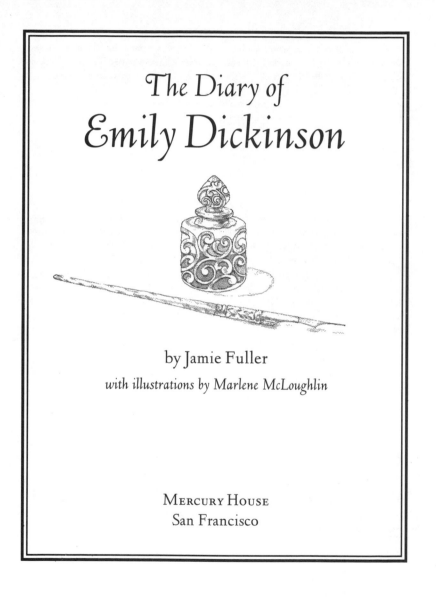

by Jamie Fuller

with illustrations by Marlene McLoughlin

MERCURY HOUSE
San Francisco

This is a work of historical fiction. With obvious exceptions, names, characters, places, and incidents either are the product of the author's imagination or are used fictitiously. Any resemblance to actual events, locales, or persons, living or dead, is entirely coincidental.

Published in the United States by
Mercury House
San Francisco, California

United States Constitution, First Amendment: Congress shall make no law respecting an establishment of religion, or prohibiting the free exercise thereof; or abridging the freedom of speech, or of the press; or the right of the people peaceably to assemble, and to petition the Government for a redress of grievances.

Mercury House and colophon are registered trademarks
of Mercury House, Incorporated

Printed on acid-free paper
Manufactured in the United States of America

Library of Congress Cataloging-in-Publication Data
Fuller, Jamie, 1945–.
  The diary of Emily Dickinson / by Jamie Fuller.
    p.   cm.
  ISBN 1-56279-048-X
    1. Dickinson, Emily, 1830–1886—Fiction.   2. Poets, American—Fiction.   I. Title.
PS3556.U445D5   1993
813'.54—dc20

                                                                          93–12728
                                                                            CIP

5   4   3   2   1

For my parents,

who made home a "holy thing"

Prologue

Wʜᴇɴ Eᴍɪʟʏ Dɪᴄᴋɪɴsoɴ ᴅɪᴇᴅ ɪɴ 1886, she left, as her gift to the world, a vast collection of poems tucked away in a locked box. It was an offering the world had little use for during her lifetime, but the apathy and incomprehension she encountered almost universally were no match for the force of her creative genius, which eventually produced the 1,800 poems now known to be in existence (1,775 in the definitive collection, 25 recently discovered and presented in what follows).

Emily's sister, Lavinia, who knew of Emily's scribblings but was unaware that they represented a lifelong passion, was astonished when she discovered the box whose contents attested to it. Whether or not she appreciated the true quality of the poems, Lavinia was unrelenting in her conviction that they must be published, if only because they were "Emily's poems." Through her persistence and the tireless editorial efforts of Mabel Loomis Todd, a family friend, the first volume, consisting of only a small portion of the total oeuvre, was published in 1890. This book went through eleven printings and was followed by a second and third series in 1891 and 1896, respectively. The reception of the poetry by critics and the public was enthusiastic for the most part, and by 1896 Emily Dickinson had gained worldwide fame. Further collections, including poems gathered from various sources, appeared over the next fifty years, but it was not until 1955 that the three-volume variorum edition—containing all 1,775 known poems and fragments, arranged chronologically (based on dating of the handwriting)—was compiled by Thomas H. Johnson and published by the Belknap Press of Harvard University Press (*The Poems of Emily Dickinson*).

After her death the world took another look at Emily Dickinson the poet and finally realized what it had been missing. Emily Dickinson the woman, however, has remained elusive. Though biographies and critical and psychoanalytical studies abound, relatively little is known about her day-to-day existence, and the limited facts bearing on her relationships with the people around her finally provide no more than food for conjecture about the true nature of those relationships. Light has been cast into some of the corners as new bits of information have emerged in recent years, but there are still as many interpretations of the "essential Emily" as there are interpreters.

We know that she was born December 10, 1830, the second of three children, into a prominent family in Amherst, Massachusetts. Her grandfather, Samuel Fowler Dickinson, was largely responsible for the founding of Amherst College, and her father, Edward, and brother, William Austin, both prosperous lawyers, continued the tradition of civic-mindedness. Emily was educated at Amherst Academy and at Mount Holyoke Female Seminary in South Hadley, where she studied only two terms before returning to Amherst to spend the rest of her life under her father's roof. Greatly attached to home, she was reluctant to leave it even for brief trips. In 1864 and 1865 she spent several months in Boston for treatment of a mysterious eye ailment, and after her return she never traveled again. In the 1860s and 1870s she became increasingly reclusive, eventually refusing to receive most visitors or to venture even as far as her brother's house next door. At some point (probably in the mid-seventies) she took to wearing white exclusively, for a reason that has never been clear, though there are many theories. There are suggestions in her letters that she was struck by the magic of poetic creation before she was twenty, though only a few poems exist that can be dated earlier than 1858. By then she had begun to write the kind of verse that would establish her reputation as perhaps the greatest American poet.

The poems provide us with insights into her thinking—her philosophies about death, immortality, love, nature, and poetry—but for the most part they offer no more than tantalizing hints of the actual events that may have served as inspiration. What information we do have about Emily's quotidian routine derives largely from the letters she wrote between 1842 and her death in 1886. All of the known letters have been collected in the three-volume *Letters of Emily Dickinson,* edited by Thomas H. Johnson and Theodora Ward (Cambridge, Mass.: Belknap Press, Harvard University Press, 1958). These volumes undoubtedly represent only a fraction of the total output, for despite her reclusiveness, Emily Dickinson had a wide circle of friends and acquaintances with whom she corresponded regularly. For her the letters were another form of artistic expression—whose language resembles that of the poems themselves. Emily's own collection of letters that she received from others was burned by Lavinia after her death, apparently on Emily's instructions.

Now at last we have a third source of information about Emily Dickinson—a diary that she kept during 1867–68, a period in her life about which hardly anything was known. Its discovery was a momentous event—but one that unfortunately was kept hidden for years while scholars struggled to fit the puzzle pieces together and admirers let their imaginations run free. The facts behind this stunning revelation are, briefly, as follows.

For most of her life Emily Dickinson resided in the house in which she was born—the brick Homestead on Main Street built by her grandfather. (Straitened circumstances led to the sale of the house in 1840 and to the Dickinson family's fifteen-year residency in a house on North Pleasant Street. Edward Dickinson bought back the Homestead in 1855.) One of Emily's favorite spots in the Main Street house was the conservatory on its east side. There she grew a variety of exotic plants that bloomed through the winter, and at a little writing desk by the window she composed many of her poems.

Martha Dickinson Bianchi, Emily's niece and the last surviving member of the family, inherited the Homestead and in 1915 sold it to the family of a local rector. The following year the house was substantially remodeled, and the conservatory was removed. As the walls of the now crumbling room were being torn down, one of the workmen chanced upon a small leatherbound book that had apparently been concealed behind a loose brick or in a crevice in the wall. By this time Emily Dickinson was a household name in Amherst. It happened that this carpenter was a lover of poetry— and hers in particular—and when he opened the little book and realized that he had found her diary, he was "seized with a violent trembling," as he later told his grandson. Both electrified and terrified by the discovery, he hid the book in his lunch bucket until the workday ended and then took it home. He told himself that after he had read and savored every page, he would turn the diary over to someone who would know how best to share it with the public. But as he read, he fell more and more deeply under the poet's spell and began to imagine that he was her confidant. He convinced himself that in his new role he was no longer obliged to give up the diary. Finally, having brushed away the light taps of conscience, he hid the book at the back of an oak chest in his bedroom, from which he would draw it out periodically over the course of the next sixty-four years until he had virtually memorized its contents. Even his family never knew of its existence.

Shortly before his death in 1980 at the age of eighty-nine, the old man finally showed his most prized possession to his grandson (his only son having preceded him in death), confessing that his delight in it had always been tempered by a nagging guilt and asking that the young man now attempt to atone for his grandfather's sin. The grandson, however, had inherited both the old man's passion for poetry and his tendency toward paralysis of conscience, and he readily succumbed to the temptation to hold onto the diary indefinitely while trying to decide what ought to be done with it. Finally, after several years and a promise of anonymity for all parties concerned, the present editor was able, through a series of convoluted channels, to obtain this priceless document. Now, after a delay of three-quarters of a century, it can be presented for the enjoyment of all Emily Dickinson admirers.

The diary is a small, dark brown book, measuring approximately five by seven inches, and containing plain pages that could have been used for any sort of writing. The entries—each identified by day and month at the top (each year designation appears only once)—are written in ink, with very few words crossed out or altered. It is possible that Emily did a pencil draft first, of some or all of the entries, as was her practice in writing poetry, but several of them suggest otherwise. The diary begins in March 1867 and ends a little more than a year later. There are 102 entries, written at apparently random intervals a few days or sometimes a week apart. The first entry gives a fairly clear statement of why Emily Dickinson decided to begin keeping a journal, but the reason for its abrupt conclusion in April 1868 is less plain. We can never know, of course, whether she intended to continue and was for some reason distracted, but the last entry does have the feel of finality. The diary gives evidence that, as Emily once commented elsewhere, "My life has been too simple and stern to embarrass any." The book is more significant as a window into her thoughts than as a detailed chronicling of events. Indeed, the first entry makes plain her intent in this regard.

As thrilling as the unearthing of the diary itself is the discovery of twenty-five previously unknown poems interspersed among the entries (bringing Emily's total known output to 1,800). These, too, appear sporadically, but each bears a relationship to the preceding entry.

In preparing the diary for publication, the editor has preserved Emily's idiosyncratic spelling and punctuation—as well as the spellings she used that were correct in her day. Numbers have been added to the diary entries to facilitate cross-referencing, and most of the entries are annotated to identify particular people and events with which the reader might not be familiar. The style of day and month has been standardized (Emily sometimes reversed the order of the two and frequently omitted the day; her usual spelling of February as "Febuary" has been corrected). Previously extant poems are referred to by the numbers given them by Thomas H. Johnson, editor of the three-volume *Poems of Emily Dickinson* (and of the one-volume *Complete Poems of Emily Dickinson,* published by Little, Brown). Some of these are referred to in the notes to particular diary entries to help elucidate the text; in such cases the numbered poem is included following the entry, as part of the commentary. The versions used here are taken from the one-volume *Complete Poems,* in which obvious misspellings (including misplaced apostrophes) have been corrected.

As might be expected, the diary touches on many of the same themes the reader finds in Emily's poems and letters—the relationship between God and humanity and the nature of faith, the shadow that death and suffering cast over daily existence, the role of romantic love in her life, and especially her sense of poetry's power over her and the sacrifices that must be made in its pursuit. These pages reveal much that was heretofore only suspected and lay to rest some erroneous surmises, but in the end Emily Dickinson will probably always remain an enigma. No doubt this was her intent. It now appears that her professed aversion to publication and its accompanying fame thinly disguised a sense of destiny and an underlying faith that her artistic achievements could not escape eventual recognition. Yet it is equally clear that she wanted future generations to know her through her art—where she "sang the World" in a way no one ever had before. The editor likes to think that Emily would not regard the publication of this "letter to herself" as an intrusion but rather as an enhancement of that incomparable melody.

J. F.

The Diary

[1]

Thursday, March 14, 1867

Today I witnessed Death defeated by a bold crocus.
Undaunted by winter's white shroud, it rose renewed
to merge in gold with the sun. Nature is recovering
– and Spring is the proof. Each year she promises
return but then lies ill so long that Hope misgives us.
Revived, we can forgive a penurious God!

Rebirth requires commemoration. Though I sing
Life – instinctively – as the Robin – I never jotted
hours. I live too quietly for Volumes – No stage
would play my Drama. But Thought is it's own
Event and defines the day. Recording one preserves
the other, like the flower pressed between pages at it's
fullest glory. So let this be my letter to myself – that
needs no response.

The last line is an echo of poem 441, "This is my letter to the World"
(following), written about 1862.

(441)
This is my letter to the World
That never wrote to Me –

13

The simple News that Nature told –
With tender Majesty

Her Message is committed
To Hands I cannot see –
For love of Her – Sweet – countrymen –
Judge tenderly – of Me

 [2]

Monday, March 18

It was baking day – which relieved me of the
necessity to participate in dustier chores! Our
friendly kitchen permits Nature's observation.
To knead to bird antics exalts the task. While my
hands work, my mind sets off for wider parts. If
it returns with treasures, I inscribe them on whatever is at hand.

 To bake a loaf is to create what had not been till
then – as a Poet makes a verse. Yet they differ – for
the Crumb may fail if Imagination gallops beyond
it's proportions – but an untrammeled spirit is the
yeast of Poetry. Bread is safer – only follow it's
prescription and acceptance is assured.

At supper tonight the multitude approved. Father
commented particularly on the crust – welcome
praise since my brown "verse" is made to please him
most. He would not care for the other!

Martha Dickinson Bianchi, Emily's niece, described the kitchen at the Homestead, the Edward Dickinson family residence, as a "cheerful place" with many windows, light green walls, and door and window casings of deep yellow. It was a wide room that extended across the back of the house. Emily had a habit of scribbling poems on any convenient scrap of paper, including recipes, when the impulse seized her.

She was responsible for most of the cooking in the Dickinson household, particularly bread baking, and preferred this task to other forms of housework. Her longtime correspondent and mentor, Thomas Wentworth Higginson, reported after meeting her in 1870, "She makes all the bread for her father only likes hers. . . ."

[3]

Wednesday, March 20

Tonight the needle exhausted my fingers – while my
mind flew away. The flight gave them no pause! I
watched the thread course through the fabric remem-
bering that other – bolder – strand which binds my

soul to Life. As a girl – when the magic of Poetry came upon me – I tried to paint it for dear Jane – a shining golden fibre that pierced my center and drew me toward a purpose I had not seen except in dreams. My words I guess were not the equal of my heart – for my friend never answered to show she understood. I knew if I could weave this fibre through my sum of days – it would make a fabric bright enough – for joy – and strong enough for anguish – a garment for the ages. Many have given their souls to God – I entrust mine to gold.

In April of 1850 Emily wrote a long letter to her friend Jane Humphrey in which she described the recent religious conversion of some of her friends and relatives as a sanctifying experience: "Christ is calling everyone here, all my companions have answered, even my darling Vinnie believes she loves, and trusts him, and I am standing alone in rebellion, and growing very careless. . . . I cant tell you *what* they have found, but *they* think it is something precious. I wonder if it *is?* How strange is this sanctification, that works such a marvellous change. . . . It *certainly* comes from God – and I think to receive it is blessed – not that I know it from *me,* but from those on whom *change* has passed."

Next to this description she juxtaposed an account of her own experience—apparently as transforming in its way as any religious awakening: "I have dared to do strange things – bold things, and have asked no advice from any – I have heeded beautiful tempters, yet do not think I am wrong. . . . Oh Jennie, it would relieve me to tell you all, to sit down at your feet, and look in your eyes, and confess what *you only* shall know, an experience bitter, and sweet, but the sweet did so beguile me – and life has had an aim, and the world has been too precious for your poor – and striving sister! . . . What do you weave from all these threads . . . bring it nearer the window, and I will see, it's all wrong unless it has one gold thread in it, a long, big shining fibre which hides the others – and which will fade away into Heaven while you hold it, and from there come back to me. . . . Nobody *thinks* of the joy, nobody *guesses* it . . . but there *now* is nothing old, things are budding, and springing, and singing, and you rather think you are in a green grove, and it's branches that go, and come."

Scholars have speculated that the "gold thread" metaphor represents Emily Dickinson's growing awareness that her life must be dedicated to poetry—which will give her an "aim." Entry No. 3 appears to bear out this interpretation.

This is the first of many entries in the diary that illustrate Emily's ambivalent attitude toward God and formal religion. Although she can legitimately be regarded as a "religious" poet—in the sense that much of her work delves into the unfathomable operation of God in human existence—she rarely attended church after her twenties and could never bring herself to submit to a formal "conversion" to the faith. All of the other members of her family did so, and in some of her girlhood letters, like the one quoted here, she expressed regret at her own reluctance. The conflict between the desire to maintain her independence from God's incomprehensible demands and her sense, as is evident in much of her poetry, of having been chosen for her task was a spiritual struggle she waged to the end of her life.

 [4]

Friday, March 22

Vinnie departed this morning for Cambridge to visit
Fanny and Loo for a few days. She has'nt the antipa-
thy to travel that keeps me contented at home. Duty
also binds me. Mother and Father would too much
feel the absence of both – Mother for comfort and
Father for habit!

But without Vinnie the house misses it's joy. We
have the closeness of spirit that comes from sisterhood
– and though our minds seek out different corners, I
am not at peace without her. Our bond is indissoluble.

Still there is a part of me I do not share with her.
She knows I write – but there is a vail between us
that blocks her full understanding of the effort. I might
divulge more but she avoids Inquiry. Whether she has
no interest in the question or fears the answer I dont
know. Perhaps she would not fully comprehend the
Music, though she might commend the playing. I
choose silence – to avoid the test.

Emily's sister, Lavinia Norcross Dickinson (called "Vinnie" by family and friends), was born in 1833, three years after Emily. Emily's existing letters, as well as letters and later reminiscences by Vinnie, are evidence of the sisters' lifelong closeness, though their natures were quite different. As Emily once observed in a letter to a friend, "if we had come up for the first time from two wells where we had hitherto been bred her astonishment would not be greater at some things I say" (quoted in Richard B. Sewall, *The Lyman Letters: New Light on Emily Dickinson and Her Family*, published by the University of Massachusetts Press, Amherst, in 1965).

But she also once commented, after reporting to a friend that Vinnie had a headache, "when the head aches next to you, it becomes important. When she is well, time leaps. When she is ill, he lags, or stops entirely.

"Sisters are brittle things. God was penurious with me, which makes me shrewd with Him."

In a letter of 1883 she used a phrase reminiscent of the one in this entry to describe her bond to Vinnie—"early, earnest, indissoluble."

See also Nos. 5, 15, 30, 36, 52, and 59.

Frances and Louise Norcross (Fanny and Loo) were the daughters of Emily's mother's sister and were seventeen and twelve years younger than Emily. Her correspondence with her "little cousins" was a lengthy and affectionate one, extending from 1859 until shortly before she died.

Saturday, March 30

My mind – rebellious – all day fled from chores
and begged me to follow. Vinnie, returned from
Cambridge yesterday, despairs at what was not
accomplished in her absence. Today she grew cross
because I neglected my portion of the mending –
and accused me of dalliance with daydreams! She
did not know that four lines had sprung full grown
from my head and cried for preservation! Dinner
was delayed because I kept the roast from the oven
too long – and Father was displeased. I dont know
whose wrath strikes more terror – Vinnie's or
Father's! But for the sake of verse I willingly incur
it! I often wish I never had to tarry for a task – but
perfect freedom would dilute a concentrated Bliss.
Our finest minutes earn their color by the depriva-
tion of preceding hours.

[6]

Sunday, March 31

Another Sunday morning – and both houses are at
services. They have forsworn urging me to attend
with them though I sometimes yield to the persua-
sion. The new pastor, Mr. Jenkins, is a powerful
orator. He somewhat reminds me of Mr. Wadsworth, who has been my faithful listener since
Philadelphia. I chose him to shape my spirit as Mr.
Higginson my words. How bold I was to suppose
they would accept the Mentor's role – and how
blessed by their acquiescence!

Though we are now separated by a continent,
I look to Mr. Wadsworth's pulpit to assuage the
doubts that never can be cured. The Mind sees the
folly but the Soul wont cease it's search.

My preacher argues that Belief is mightier than
Proof. When I ask – what are we to God? – he
affirms – in a loud voice – his faith in that Design
all men seek and none can find. There is certainty in
my friend's words but I sense disquiet in his heart.
"In wisdom is grief and he that increaseth knowledge

increaseth sorrow." Perhaps the questions give him
strength to frame the answers – and his vigorous
replies muffle his own Doubts.

After a visit in 1855 to Washington, D.C., where Edward Dickinson was serving as a United States congressman from Massachusetts, Emily and Vinnie spent two weeks in Philadelphia with family friends. It was on this occasion that Emily is presumed to have met the Reverend Charles Wadsworth, minister of the Arch Street Presbyterian Church, an assumption borne out by this entry, and to have begun a correspondence that lasted until Wadsworth's death in 1882. (At the time of this writing he had moved to Calvary Church in San Francisco.)

None of Emily's letters to Wadsworth survive and only one of his to her—an undated message that misspells her name and expresses sympathy over some undesignated "sorrow." A sense of what Wadsworth meant to her comes largely from her letters to his friends James and Charles Clark, written after his death. In one she refers to him as her "Shepherd from 'Little Girl'hood," but it is also apparent from the questions she asked the Clarks that she knew little about his personal life. Only two meetings between them are known to have taken place—in 1860 and 1880.

For more on the Wadsworth/Dickinson relationship, see No. 49.

For a note on Higginson, see No. 8.

Jonathan Jenkins was pastor of the First Congregational Church in Amherst from December 1866 until 1877, when he and his family moved to Pittsfield. They remained close to the Dickinsons even after their move. A son, MacGregor Jenkins, has written an account of Emily Dickinson as he remembered her from childhood in *Emily Dickinson: Friend and Neighbor* (Boston: Little, Brown, 1930).

The quoted sentence in the last paragraph of this entry paraphrases the King James version of Ecclesiastes 1:18. (Emily's quotations are seldom exact.)

"Why" is what we cannot know –
"Where" the place we cannot go
Before the Summons come –
Pale creeds tremble to explain
Postulations never seen
Until we stumble Home.

Pulpits powerless to limn
Merest edges of a scheme
Wider than the eye –
For a weapon counsel prayer,
Efficacious more than spear –
Battling Divinity.

Polar Death would never freeze
Souls cloaked in contenter days
Did we understand –

The dimensions of the Game –
Whence the arrow, where the aim
Of that mighty Hand.

 [7]

Friday, April 5

A day of culinary frustration! This morning I had
just put Father's favorite pudding in the oven when
called to the side door by a child looking for his lost
pussy. I let my attention fix on his plight and took
him to the barn – where there is much amusement
for a cat! Our search was long but unsuccessful and
when I returned the pudding was burned. Not
wishing to disappoint Father, I made a second batch.
Later I put potatoes on to boil but let the pan run
dry while I took a respit from my watch. Some lines
occurred and I had no pencil handy. I hurried to the
conservatory but forgot to hurry back! Caution
finally found me – and the rest of the dinner reached
uneventful completion.

Housewifery is wearisome – but Devotion shapes the task. As we all sat at table – so different in our longings and secret sorrows yet joined by Love's mysterious adhesive power – I thought again how holy a place is home. For though we share meals more easily than minds, in no other ground could my seeds take root. Here no man times my toil and I answer to none for it. Though I must do my part for the family's comforts, yet I have the freedom – and solitude – for my truest work – such as a wife would never know.

There is safety in their familiar affection – demonstrated warily. To ask for understanding were – perhaps – ingratitude.

In a letter to her brother, Austin, written after he returned to his teaching job in Boston following a brief visit home in October 1851, Emily wrote: "Home is a holy thing – nothing of doubt or distrust can enter it's blessed portals."

8

Wednesday, April 10

*The birds woke me before dawn and the day cried
for song. My thoughts rushed about but would not
form a row. I turned instead to breakfast – to give
them time to muster. Later – while the bread baked
– I put my hand again to the page – where once
more it met resistance. Then I felt the familiar fright
– that stabs my heart when there is no sound to
shape the sense. Once I knew a larger terror – that
– even after molding – Thought might remain numb.
When that Doubt arose – like a demon – it seemed
to split me from myself and ruled my days. Then I
turned to Mr. Higginson – for I thought he would
show me the truth. I could not weigh myself – and
trembled lest others' scales report no gravity. If my
purpose were gossamer, what had I to cling to? How
does one live without an Aim?*

*He was kind and told me to continue – and
though he usually seeks to pare he often praises too.
Now if the world be deaf – or turn from the Melody*

– I happily sing on. To know one faithful listener
bears me home. Silence were death – and he saved
my life.

In April 1862 Emily read an article in the *Atlantic Monthly*, entitled "Letter to a Young Contributor," written by Thomas Wentworth Higginson, a noted man of letters, former Unitarian minister, abolitionist, and commander of a black regiment in South Carolina during the Civil War. The article, offering advice to would-be writers seeking to have their work published, inspired one of Emily's most famous letters. On April 15, 1862, she wrote to Higginson, enclosing four of her poems and asking, "Are you too deeply occupied to say if my Verse is alive?"

Higginson apparently replied at once to her query, asking for more information about her, which she provided in her usual cryptic fashion in a letter of April 25. It was in this letter that she told Higginson, "I had a terror – since September – I could tell to none – and so I sing, as the Boy does by the Burying Ground – because I am afraid – ." The source of the "terror" to which she referred has continued to baffle readers of the letter to this day, with suggested solutions to the riddle ranging from the loss of a lover to a fear that she was going blind (she was in fact treated for some unknown eye trouble but not until 1864–65, and it evidently did not harm her vision).

This diary entry now makes clear that the clue to the "terror" can be found in the April 25 letter itself. There Emily, thanking Higginson for his "surgery" in critiquing her poems, remarked, "I bring you others – as you ask – though they might not differ –

"While my thought is undressed – I can make the distinction, but when I put them in the Gown – they look alike, and numb."

In entry No. 8 she specifically refers to a "larger terror" of some earlier time—that her poetic efforts might remain "numb" and her life be rendered essentially purposeless as a result. (See No. 3 dealing with the "gold thread" imagery.) Though the metaphor here is musical ("sound") rather than sartorial ("put them in the Gown"), the logical inference is that both writings describe the same emotional crisis.

No. 8 also contains other echoes of the April 25 letter. There she explained, "I could not weigh myself – Myself –

"My size felt small – to me – I read your Chapters in the Atlantic – and experienced honor for you – I was sure you would not reject a confiding question – ."

In 1869 Emily wrote to Higginson, "You were not aware that you saved my Life."

The 1862 inquiry began a rather curious correspondence between the poet and the critic, lasting until Emily's death, in which she continued to send Higginson samples of her work, always regarding him as her mentor ("I had no Monarch in my life"), and he continued to respond while considering her poems too far afield of contemporary poetic conventions to be acceptable for publication. It was not until after her death, when he assisted Mrs. Todd in the publication of the poems, that Higginson began to appreciate their quality.

For additional insight into the relationship, see Nos. 17, 39, 58, and 82.

9

Saturday, April 13

Here is todays harvest. Tomorrow I shall send it over the hedge to Sue – though I am half fearful to do so. She has always been kind to receive and comment on my verse though like the others I doubt she suspects what Creation is to me. Once she showed a larger enthusiasm for the role of critic – but now she has less time for Thought. She is much in demand as a hostess and fulfills that role beyond all others. To be the center of radiance suits her for she has a brilliant mind and a rare charm that does not detract from it. But there is some void she seeks to fill with the company and conversation of others. Domestic pleasures do not satisfy –

Sue's friendship is still a gem to me but the crack between us widens with the years. The bond of girlhood has loosened – I thought us inseparable then but perhaps the cord was never so tight around her heart as mine.

My sister I name her still – and always will – but we glimpse each other through a shadow.

Susan Gilbert, a childhood friend of Emily's, married Emily's brother, Austin, in 1856, a match that Emily apparently encouraged. Existing documents (particularly the reminiscences of Mabel Loomis Todd, who became Austin's lover in the 1880s) suggest that it was a rocky marriage (see No. 20).

Susan Dickinson was a bright light in society, and her home was renowned as the setting for frequent gatherings of luminaries such as Ralph Waldo Emerson. Maintaining this social role evidently became Sue's raison d'être, though, as indicated here, she was also a woman of considerable intelligence and took enough interest in Emily's poetry to offer frequent criticism of it.

There are suggestions in Emily's notes and letters to Sue, as well as in some of her poems and in later comments by various observers, of a growing rift between the two, a conclusion that has been accepted by most scholars. Their across-the-hedge correspondence continued until the end of Emily's life, however, and as late as 1882 she paid Sue a cryptic compliment: "With the exception of Shakespeare, you have told me of more knowledge than any one living – To say that sincerely is strange praise."

The poem that follows this entry was not found among Sue's large collection of Emily's verses, which was eventually published by Martha Dickinson Bianchi. It cannot now be known whether the copy was lost or whether Emily changed her mind and never passed the poem along to Sue.

The day is but a Preface
Insinuating awe
Revealed in fuller Document,
Half open to our view –

Astounded – first – by Morning,
We turn the page to Noon –
And tremble at the starry close
Of Nature's Lexicon –

Each syllable as startling
As blaze of sudden fire –
The reading of that Majesty
Reclaims a faithless hour.

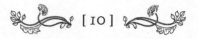

Thursday, April 18

Tonight as we tidied the kitchen after supper, Vinnie
stepped outside with some table scraps for the pussies.
Suddenly she called my name in a tone that drew me
to the door. I looked out just in time to see a golden
tail streak across the purple horizon. "It's a shooting
star!" Vinnie exclaimed – and indeed it appeared to
be though it passed so quickly I almost thought our
eyes deceived us. Mother heard us and hurried in
but was too late to witness the event. The speedy
courier – bound for some foreign destination – never
tarried but bore his message on. Our view – perhaps
– was accidental – and we must glean the purpose
from the passage. "There are more things in heaven"
than we can conceive.

The weekly Amherst newspaper, the *Hampshire Express,* reported in its
April 25 edition that on Thursday, April 18, about 7:30 P.M. "a very brilliant
meteor was seen in the Northwestern sky."

The quote is from *Hamlet,* act 1, scene 5.

[II]

Morning came with reluctance – and the sky still
mingles tears with hope. We like a vivid Easter –
but Nature – remembering the first – chooses a more
fitting compromise. The family are at church – where
presumptuous bonnets vie with Faith – but I prefer
to spend this morning with my Bible – to hear again
the story of that Day – that taught us how to suffer.
The Gospels promise permanence but remind us of
our evanescence. Even he who died for Truth – the
greatest blasphemy – could not escape fulfillment of
that ageless Prophecy.

We read the tale – admonishing the Followers –
but the cock crows many times in our hearts and
Thomas sets our example. Faith itself is our cross –
We stumble under it's weight but cannot put it
down. How much lighter the step of those who do
not bear the seeker's burden.

Sabachthani – at the Ninth Hour –
In that assuageless cry
Was pain enough to unmoor worlds,
Wrench continents away

The whisper was a Summons –
The Agony a gift –
The Death demise of Certainty –
All Doctrines set adrift!

The spiteful succor offered
In vinegar and gall –
And then a Soaring upward –
Atonement for the Fall.

Thursday, April 25

The days are lengthening at summer's approach –
and dusk repeats the Dawn. Now at suppertime –
while I stir – my kitchen window surpasses Titian.
Tonight I trembled as the western sky kindled the
trees and purple flames devoured the horizon. Our
eye is too small to surround the Awe. Has the Soul
a larger vision? Are we "part or parcel" of that
mighty Conflagration – or only helpless witnesses
to it's confounding Colors?

The quoted words may be an allusion to the following passage from Ralph Waldo Emerson's essay "Nature": "Standing on the bare ground,—my head bathed by the blithe air and uplifted into infinite space,—all mean egotism vanishes. I become a transparent eyeball; I am nothing; I see all; the currents of the Universal Being circulate through me; I am part or parcel of God."

The extent to which Emily Dickinson was influenced by Emerson's transcendentalist philosophy has been the subject of much scholarly speculation. Additional references appear in Nos. 25 and 66.

Dawn ignites the sky
To confound the eye –
Not to praise –
That we share the Source –
Or conceive – the Force –
Of the Blaze

His inciting spark
Rectifying dark
Lessens proof
That the Mystery
Of Divinity –
Is Ourself.

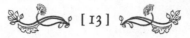

13

Saturday, April 27

*I walked next door this afternoon to return a book
to Sue – hoping to thank her personally for the
lending – but she was not at home. I found Clara
practicing Mozart and stayed to listen – for she
creates sounds of particular sweetness. My piano
was once a daily delight – but I seldom play now.
Life cant hold the hours – and my Soul makes room
for other Glory. Words have become my notes and
Wonder the keyboard. Now I "sing a new song."
Truth is the finest Melody – adherent as a Hymn
in a willing ear.*

The Evergreens, home of Emily's brother, Austin, and his family, was
located to the west of the Homestead. Clara and Anna Newman were the
daughters of Edward Dickinson's sister Mary and became his wards after
they were orphaned in 1852. They came to live at the Evergreens in 1858
and remained until Clara's marriage in 1869.

Emily played the square carved piano in the Homestead parlor as a girl
and into womanhood but eventually withdrew from the keyboard—at
least by 1867, as this entry indicates. Clara notes in her reminiscences that
Emily enjoyed hearing her play.

For more on Clara, see No. 41.

The quotation is from Psalms 96:1.

A poem is music
Played upon the Soul –
Divinely strung,
Vibrating out of will –
It shapes Life,
As the staff defines the note,
By the restrainless harmony of Thought
That sings the World
In an immortal key –
Imagination is my Symphony!

 [14]

Wednesday, May 1

Looking in my mirror tonight – I saw – as for the
first time – a face that seldom draws my attention.
Certainly it never made the world turn round. It
reminds me of the sparrow – a dun creature scorned
by it's fellows of more brilliant plumage but given
still it's role in nature's drama. I try to stun with
words – but the world prefers harmonious features.
I had my image captured once – in girlhood – but

though Father beseeches – since then I have declined
to fix myself within a frame – unless it be the
confines of a verse! The artificial does not satisfy. I
would not displease Father – but I am the better
portrait – if only he would look more closely.

Only one photograph of Emily Dickinson is known to exist, a picture taken when she was about seventeen that does indeed reveal a woman whose features do not "stun."

Early in the correspondence between Emily and Higginson, he apparently asked her for a picture. She responded, "Could you believe me – without? I had no portrait, now, but am small, like the Wren, and my Hair is bold, like the Chestnut Bur – and my eyes, like the Sherry in the Glass, that the Guest leaves – Would this do just as well?

"It often alarms Father – He says Death might occur, and he has Molds of all the rest – but has no Mold of me, but I noticed the Quick wore off those things, in a few days, and forestall the dishonor – You will think no caprice of me – ."

After his first meeting with Emily in 1870, Higginson described her in a letter to his wife: "A step like a pattering child's in entry & in glided a little plain woman with two smooth bands of reddish hair & a face . . . with no good feature – in a very plain & exquisitely clean white pique & blue net worsted shawl." But Emily's niece, Martha Bianchi, later insisted that if she had "no good feature," neither did she have any bad one.

The complex relationship between Emily and her father, hinted at in this entry, is developed more fully in the rest of the diary.

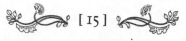

Monday, May 6

This was the day Vinnie had chosen to commence
the spring cleaning. She has resolved that every nook
must be swept, the least ornament dusted, the
curtains aired, and the mattresses turned – and for
good measure she will rearrange the pantry – which
seems content as it is! We have'nt a girl at present,
but Vinnie vows to accomplish the feat herself – with
my assistance in the tasks she assigns – and I dont
doubt she can.

   She amuses me with her household enthusiasms –
because they never enticed me. Disorder in the parlor
so discomforts her that she will not rest until it is
set right! I am content to follow her instructions.
Housewifely pursuits are mostly tedium to me –
except as respit from devouter labors.

   Progress was made – we have beaten and swept
to exhaustion – but I fear several days remain before
Vinnie "pronounces it good." The pantry waits
patiently, beckoning to us from Friday. For Vinnies
sake I feign vigor though I guess I cant fool her!

The toil has left me stripped of inspiration. This is all my pen can do today.

Between 1865 and 1869 the Dickinsons had a succession of different housemaids. This account must have been written during an interval when they were without one.

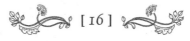 [16]

Wednesday, May 8

This early evening, the supper chores completed,
I passed a pleasant hour with Mrs. Browning. In
her presence I feel the strength of Poetry – and a
woman's power. How honestly she translates the
heart and therefore Life itself. Poets are the "only
truth-tellers," but Truth is no servant to sex.
    She came late to love – and her sonnets are
evidence that Bliss postponed remunerates the delay.
I have knocked – timid – at Love's door but only
Poetry gave me admittance. Passion's silhouette is all
I know. Yet it is coeval with Creation – the piercing

*of the spirit – and Imagination is the poet's province.
To know the one is to suppose the other.*

*Aurora Leigh did not find love till she became the
mistress of her soul. Men and women have their
boundaries. Happy those who learn to cross them
freely. The unions ordained by Nature come easily –
to most – when Fate is generous. But can one soul
enter another? To merge mind with mind were
utterest consummation.*

Elizabeth Barrett Browning was probably Emily's favorite woman writer.
Browning was born in 1806 and died in 1861. She achieved fame as a poet
in her own right before marrying the equally famous poet Robert Browning in 1846 at the age of forty. Their own love story was the inspiration for
much of her later poetry, including *Sonnets from the Portuguese* and the
verse novel *Aurora Leigh,* which she completed in 1856.

Emily knew *Aurora Leigh* well and alluded to it a number of times in her
letters. It is the story of a young woman who turns away from the conventional role reserved for her sex in the nineteenth century to devote her life
to poetry. She refuses an offer of marriage from her cousin Romney, who
professes to love her but has little sympathy for her ambition. Aurora
eventually achieves fame as a poet and is reunited with Romney, whose
character and attitudes have changed during the course of a difficult life.
He and Aurora finally come to a fuller appreciation of each other.

Emily was evidently deeply impressed by the ability of a strong woman, as exemplified in both Aurora Leigh and her creator, to fulfill her poetic ambitions without having to compromise them in the attainment of love.

The quotation in the first paragraph is from a line in *Aurora Leigh* describing poets as "the only truth-tellers now left to God" (1, 859).

In a poem written about 1873, "To pile like Thunder to its close" (1247), Emily equates love and poetry in a manner that recalls paragraph two of this entry.

(1247)
To pile like Thunder to its close
Then crumble grand away
While Everything created hid
This – would be Poetry –

Or Love – the two coeval come –
We both and neither prove –
Experience either and consume –
For None see God and live –

Friday, May 10

Today's post brought another letter from Mr.
Higginson, my tireless Preceptor. He finds the last
verse I sent him "rich" in imagery but urges more
attention to rhyme.

For the past five years I have much valued his
surgery but still his knife does not find the mark.
He has always quarreled with my form and begs me
to smooth it – but that would be diminuendo – and
I must sing at full voice. As to content, he finds it
"leans to the unfathomable" but that is Life itself.
I do not know the source of the Music – only that I
cannot alter the tune.

I ask Mr. Higginson for advice – because it were
folly to only write and hide. But I am powerless to
take it – seeking an affirmation he will not give.
He tries to listen but cannot hear – yet the effort
endears him to me. We are bound by love of the
written word – and though our minds miss their
junction, yet our paths run parallel. It needs but one
small bending toward the fork – and I believe at last
we shall meet at the center.

See No. 8, which describes the beginning of the Dickinson/Higginson relationship. In her second letter to Higginson, dated April 25, 1862, Emily, apparently responding to his comments on the first four poems she had sent him, thanked him for "the surgery – it was not so painful as I supposed."

Although she always valued the correspondence, Emily apparently ignored most of Higginson's surgical efforts, as her poetry attests. As she explained in a letter of June 7, 1862, "I thanked you for your justice – but could not drop the Bells whose jingling cooled my Tramp – ." This diary entry, along with Nos. 8, 39, 58, and 82, does, however, shed some light on their baffling relationship.

There is no clue here to the particular poem referred to in the first paragraph. (Most of the Dickinson oeuvre would fit the description.) She may have been speaking of one of the poems that precede this entry in the diary.

[18]

Monday, May 13

May is contagious. Let one branch or bird begin to swell with newness – and all of Nature revels in mimicry! We read that Boston is aglow with the season's magnificence. Amherst too "brings forth her bud" as a "bride adorned with jewels." The trees are decked in green-gold filigrane and the lawns –

bestrewn with flowers – are brilliant as Persia! The sounds of Earth are audible in the grass – and Heaven in the air.

Thus is our spirit of heaviness made lighter by these garments of praise. Life makes us wait for what may never come – and yearning cant speed arrival – but Spring repays our trust. Though the delay be painful, release comes at last.

The allusions here are to Isaiah 61, verses 10 and 11 in the first paragraph and verse 3 in the second.

[19]

Thursday, May 16

Chores stole the day and I had no chance to peruse the Express until late this evening. In the usual column I found an amusing poem – "A Lawyer's Ode to Spring" – a paean to spring couched in legal language. I cut it for my collection. Surrounded by the law, I am no stranger to the tongue. But it gives an odd shape to Spring!

I always look forward to reading the weekly
poems. The words are smoothly ordered, as would
please Mr. Higginson – but I speak Life differently.
Sometimes I imagine lines of my own rising bold
from the page until the thought control itself.

Mr. Higginson counsels against publication – but
I have often told him that print does not entice me.
Why should I seek others to praise my verse since I
am compelled to sing by a Force no Audience can
alter. If my Tune is not to the World's taste – let us
find our separate Harmonies. This thought I put on
the page – but in it's stillest moments the Soul
whispers, Does Melody unheard deserve it's name?

The poem referred to here appeared in the regular poetry column on the
first page of the *Hampshire Express* for May 16, 1867, and is reproduced on
the next page.

No. 19 clearly shows Emily's ambivalence about the idea of publish-
ing her poems. (Eleven were in fact published during her lifetime but
all apparently without her express consent.) Although she insisted to
Higginson that she had no interest in publication ("I smile when you suggest that I delay 'to publish' – that being foreign to my thought, as Firmament to Fin – "), there is much evidence elsewhere in her writing to suggest that she hoped for an eventual audience—even if it could not be in
her lifetime. In fact, the sentence that follows "Firmament to Fin" in the

Higginson letter hints at this ambition: "If fame belonged to me, I could not escape her – if she did not, the longest day would pass me on the chase – . . . " It is hard to imagine how fame could have "belonged" to her had her poems never seen print.

In 1861 she wrote to her sister-in-law, "Could I make you and Austin – proud – sometime – a great way off – 'twould give me taller feet – ."

See also Nos. 78 and 101.

The third sentence of the entry gives support to the suggestion of some scholars that Emily kept a file of newspaper clippings.

A LAWYER'S ODE TO SPRING

(Reprinted from New York Evening Gazette)

Whereas, on certain boughs and sprays,
Now divers birds are heard to sing,
And certain flowers their heads upraise,
Hail to the coming on of spring!

The songs of those said birds arouse
The memory of our youthful hours—
As green as those said sprays and boughs,
As fresh and sweet as those said flowers.

The birds aforesaid—happy pairs!—
Love 'mid the aforesaid boughs enshrines
In freehold nest, themselves, their heirs,
Administrators and assigns.

Oh! busiest term of Cupid's court,
Where tender plaintiffs action bring—
Season of frolic and of sport—
Hail, as aforesaid, coming spring!

Saturday, May 18

Tonight Sue arrived at our door when supper was
scarcely finished. Her face wore a look of such
disquiet – my heart could not but slow from sorrow
for her. She said little to us excepting Father –
whom she persuaded to give her audience in his
library. There she finds a ready source of sympathy.
They discoursed privately for a long while before she
finally left.

   I suppose it was another disagreement with
Austin that incited her flight to us. Theirs was no
heaven-made union – and marriage must contain a
<u>bit</u> of heaven – or be swallowed by it's opposite! As
girls we dreamed of that quiet yielding – love's
mysterious companion – but hoped to keep our inner
lives unbowed. Now I think Sue finds burdensome in
marriage that which should most delight – She
always wished to fly but her early choice has bound
her to the nest. Perhaps it could not be otherwise –
for womanhood demands too much. I never had to
make her choice. As a girl I had a few admirers –
but it was more wit than woman that drew them.

*Now – in unsought moments – my senses
wrestle with the choice – of poetry or love – But I
know where victory must lie. Surrender of the heart
were brief – unless there be a truce of equals.*

As pointed out in the note to No. 9, the marriage between Susan and Austin Dickinson was not a happy one. The two were far different in personality and background. Sue, the daughter of an Amherst tavernkeeper, was reared by relatives in Geneva, New York, after her mother died when she was seven; her father died in poverty when she was eleven. After that she spent part of her time in Geneva and part in Amherst, where she stayed with her married sister and brother-in-law.

Sue had an inordinate fear of childbirth and a consequent distaste for the physical side of marriage. According to Mrs. Todd, she induced several abortions before the birth of her first child.

Despite her marital difficulties, however, Sue's relationship with her father-in-law was always a close and affectionate one.

In June 1852 Emily wrote a letter to her future sister-in-law, whom she had not seen for a year, recounting a visit the previous evening with Sue's sister Mattie: "I walked home with Mattie . . . and wished for you, and Heaven. You did not come, Darling, but a bit of Heaven did, or so it *seemed* to us, as we walked side by side and wondered if that great blessedness which may be our's sometime, is granted now, to some. Those unions, my dear Susie, by which two lives are one, this sweet and strange adoption wherein we can but look, and are not yet admitted, how it can fill the heart, and make it gang wildly beating, how it will take *us* one day, and make us all it's own, and we shall not run away from it, but lie still and be happy!

"... I have always hoped to know if you had no dear fancy, illumining all your life, no one of whom you murmured in the faithful ear of night ... and when you come home, Susie, we must speak of these things."

In addition to this girlish passion, the letter also reflects Emily's uncertainty about the desirability of marriage: "How dull our lives must seem to the bride, and the plighted maiden, whose days are fed with gold, and who gathers pearls every evening; but to the *wife*, Susie, sometimes the *wife forgotten*, our lives perhaps seem dearer than all others in the world...." This dichotomy is a pervasive theme in her poems and letters, as well as in the diary (see, for example, No. 16).

Emily socialized with a number of male friends in her late teens and early twenties, including several Amherst College students and associates in her father's law office, but as far as is known, she formed no lasting romantic attachment to any of them.

[21]

Sunday, May 19

Early Sunday morning – I have just returned from a walk and there is still time before I must start the breakfast. The pace of the household slows on Sunday and our requirements are less urgent.

Out of doors the dewy dawn is silent as a prayer. Perhaps it is a prayer – and the voices raised from the pews a few hours hence but feeble imitation. God is more visible in the Day than at the Altar. I do not pray often – in the way understood by men. "For your Father knoweth what things you have need of before you ask Him." Does He then heed a prayer if the Answer is previous? If God chooses us and not we Him, confession of Faith were idle.

For daily prayer I substitute a poem, which is a like communion with the unfathomable – my Pen a balm that heals estrangement.

The quotation is from Matthew 6:8.

I was no more afraid to speak
To God than he to me
When at the bridge I met him
For a solemn Colloquy.

But tongue defaulted – I could only
Tremble – for – the Word –
And when the audience was done –
I knew not – what I heard!

Tuesday, May 21

I spent an hour this afternoon with my Lexicon –
and it's amazing inhabitants. When I open the book
– they seem to cry out – demanding audience for
their story. What a noble task was Mr. Webster's –
to build a single house for such variety.

Words are my truest friends – I can always turn
to them for comfort. They do not fear the Mind's
inciting acts. Though we struggle – and I begin to
fear their disobedience – they always allow me the
final mastery – which is mightier for the travail.

Their power is stupendous. It were a crime to use
them commonly. Words give breath to Thought –
and Life itself. With them we shape the world – and
taste Immortality.

Mr. Webster pronounces language the "immediate
gift of God." But does God also choose how we shall
use it?

Emily's "Lexicon" was Noah Webster's *American Dictionary of the English
Language,* published in 1828. Webster viewed his compilation of this great

work as a religious undertaking—an attempt to imbue the English language with definitions that reflected Christian values. In his introduction to the dictionary, in a section entitled "Origin of Language," Webster writes, "we may infer that language was bestowed on Adam . . . by supernatural power; or in other words, was of divine origin; for . . . we cannot admit as probable, or even possible, that he should have invented . . . even a barren language, as soon as he was created, without supernatural aid. . . . It is therefore probable that *language* as well as the faculty of speech, was the *immediate gift of God*."

In her second letter to Higginson, Emily declared, "When a little Girl, I had a friend, who taught me Immortality – but venturing too near, himself – he never returned – Soon after, my Tutor, died – and for several years, my Lexicon – was my only companion – ." As with most aspects of Emily Dickinson's life, mystery prevails; thus one can do no more than guess the identities of the persons referred to in this statement. Probably one of them was her friend Ben Newton (see No. 66).

 [23]

Thursday, May 23

Tonight while clearing the table I dropped a dish
half full of gravy – and some splashed upon Father.
For several moments Christian charity departed –
and I was <u>severely</u> upbraided for my carelessness.
"Daughter, does your mind always reside in separate
quarters from the task at hand?" I could not think

his anger unjust – he trades in justice all the day!
His patience had been stretched by strenuous hours
in the courthouse – so I said a word or two to
soothe him.

Father is stern – but he is thunder without
lightning. We guard ourselves more tightly when the
walls tremble but fear no harm from errant bolts!
Tomorrow shows no scar.

It takes both dark and light to make a household.
We are a checkered family. But life without contrast
were a sallow creature!

The severe and forbidding character of Edward Dickinson, a prominent Amherst lawyer and civic leader, has been emphasized by many biographers, but the affectionate, almost jocular, way in which Emily speaks of him in many of her letters—and in this entry—belies the conclusion that he was a household tyrant who ruled his family through intimidation. His sudden death in 1874 affected her deeply; for several years afterward she spoke of the sorrowful event as though it had only recently occurred.

As a number of the diary entries suggest, Emily's father was not a warm or confiding person, nor did he and his daughter always (or even usually) see eye to eye (she wrote to Austin in 1851, "Fathers real life and *mine* sometimes come into collision"), but on a deeper level the two appear to have shared a genuine, if unspoken, understanding.

Vinnie once described her father as "the only one to say 'damn.' Someone in every family ought to say damn of course" (from Millicent Todd

Bingham, *Emily Dickinson's Home: Letters of Edward Dickinson and His Family,* published by Harper, New York, in 1955).

Millicent Todd Bingham, daughter of Mabel Loomis Todd, recounts an anecdote in which Edward asked whether he must always be given the same chipped plate at meals. Emily thereafter took the plate to the garden and smashed it on a stone to remind herself not to give it to him again.

For further biographical details about Edward Dickinson, see the note to No. 47.

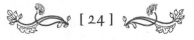

[24]

Saturday, May 25

I was dreaming – feathery thoughts that flee on naming – when I felt dawn touch my shoulder. The gray behind the curtains grew paler – A branch took shape – and suddenly Morning forced it's way into my bedchamber. Delight overwhelmed me and I could not resist. The Soul – aroused – knows how to respond. Eager for the day I take my pen. God and I are busy at depicting while the World sleeps.

I like to shape a day
As if it were a verse –
And regulate the foot
To underline the cause –
Then when the form is cast –
I polish it to gleam –
And place it with the rest
Assembled in Love's room

[25]

Monday, May 27

Vinnie and I looked after Ned and Mattie this
afternoon. The Newmans were given leave to visit
their sister for a few days and Sue has compelling
occupations. We find more joy than obligation in the
charge – for are we not instructed to suffer the little
children? Ned is full of self-importance and Mattie
of wonder. They count neither past nor future – The
Present contents them utterly. Watching their tender
trusting faces makes me solemn – when I consider
the fickleness of Possibility. Life adds weight to
innocence but it's mystery feathers the soul. How I

wish I might know their tomorrows and shield them
from the darkness. But they have their angels in
heaven. "The sun illuminates a man's eye but lights
both eye and heart of a child." Are children nearer to
God, having so recently arrived from Him? Proxim-
ity is fugitive – and frightening. We are more
comfortable with distance.

Clara and Anna Newman had two older sisters, Catherine and Sara, who lived with other families. (For more on the Newmans, see the note to No. 13.)

In May 1867, Austin and Sue's first child, Edward ("Ned") was not quite six years old. Their daughter, Martha ("Mattie"), born the previous November, was about six months old. Ned, an epileptic, died in 1898. Martha Dickinson Bianchi, the last survivor of the family, became a writer herself and chronicled the life of her famous aunt in *Emily Dickinson Face to Face: Unpublished Letters with Notes and Reminiscences* (Boston: Houghton Mifflin, 1932) and *The Life and Letters of Emily Dickinson* (Boston: Houghton Mifflin, 1924). She died in 1943.

The Dickinsons' third child, Gilbert, was born in 1875 and died of typhoid fever in 1883 not long after his eighth birthday.

The first biblical allusion in this entry is to Mark 10:14; the second, to Matthew 18:10. The last quotation is apparently a loose rendering of a sentence from Emerson's "Nature": "The sun illuminates only the eye of the man, but shines into the eye and the heart of the child." (References to Emerson also appear in Nos. 12 and 66.)

Wednesday, May 29

Mr. Bowles writes that he will come to us in June
to find refreshment in the summer air of Amherst.
My heart – as always – is unsteady at the thought
and breath draws back. The body cant forget when
it befriended the mind – to bear it's portion of despair. But now the mind – recovered – may stand
without companion.

I knew Sam – name I never dared to speak! – as
friend because he was to Austin, but fascination
overtook me and I lost my footing. Then I plunged to
love and anguish past imagining.

It was in summer at our Commencement tea
that I let my heart deceive me. There we talked until
the minutes had no measure – and I felt our bond
grow tighter, compressing breath and with it reason.
I thought he felt it too – and knew recountless
ecstasy. I knew I could not touch him but with words
– for he had chosen his companion – and those ties
are sacred. And so I sought his understanding – of
love the shining symbol – and I would be content.

But a rope stretched beyond capacity must break.
I grew too bold – When I tried to tell him of my joy
– and learn if he had love for me or what I made –
the words escaped intent. They grabbed at hidden
thoughts – rushing wildly here and there. Then I
saw the terror in his eyes. It was like a bullet
through my heart – that dared to fly without a
compass. Opening myself – I spilled my gems before
him but he found no brilliancy. Though we shared –
many words – I never lingered in his thoughts
longer than my Art – which never stopped there.

But I had a world to speak – and so I put my
love in letters – I never planned to send – to let the
page absorb the pain. The striving of the heart for
something so beyond it exhausted me – Then I
seemed to hear a faint chastising whisper, Euterpe
cannot live with Eros. The choice was too large for
me – then – and almost tore my soul in two. But
wiser years have brought a peace that quelled the
body's ache. My double Aim is not forgotten – but
now – the single is sufficient transport.

Those early days – cost me much – but they were
small to him and never dimmed our friendship.

In 1955 the complete text of three draft letters written by Emily Dickinson to an unspecified "Master," which had been discovered on her death, were finally made available by Millicent Todd Bingham in *Emily Dickinson's Home: Letters of Edward Dickinson and His Family* (New York: Harper, 1955). Until now, the identity of the person to whom these fervent love letters were addressed has remained a mystery, though strenuous arguments have been made on behalf of two of the men of Emily's acquaintance—the Presbyterian minister Charles Wadsworth and Samuel Bowles, the widely known and well-traveled editor of the *Springfield Republican*. Nor has it ever been known whether the letters were in fact sent. This diary entry now confirms that Bowles was indeed the subject of the letters and that they were never intended for mailing. Emily's confession here underscores both the complex nature of her affection for Bowles and his inability to understand it. Austin Dickinson, a good friend of Bowles, asserted after Emily's death that she had loved him "beyond sentimentality."

Because of their importance in Emily Dickinson lore and the special insight they provide into the workings of her mind and heart, all three Master letters are reproduced as part of this commentary.

Bowles became a regular visitor to the Evergreens and Homestead and a cherished friend of the Dickinson families starting about 1858. The exact circumstances under which the friendship developed are not known. Thirty-five of Emily's letters to him survive, along with thirty-seven poems that she included with them, possibly in the hope that he would take her seriously as a writer and even publish her work (though she several times disclaimed any interest in publication—see Nos. 19 and 78).

Bowles, however, appears to have been incapable of appreciating Emily Dickinson's talents. His taste ran to sentimental conventional verse heavy with melancholy—the type that regularly appeared in the *Republican* ("Nora is dying, as well as the year, / And mine is the sad, sweet task / To smooth her pillow and sit by her side, / And tell what her soft eyes ask"). Newspapers, according to his biographer, were his "chief literary food."

In April of 1862 Bowles set sail on one of his frequent trips to Europe, and Emily evidently missed him greatly. She wrote to his wife, Mary, with whom she was also in the habit of corresponding, "When the Best is gone – I know that other things are not of consequence – The Heart wants what it wants – or else it does not care – ." Although the ostensible purpose of these words was to provide comfort, it seems clear, particularly in light of this diary entry, that they had a double meaning.

Most scholars have found signs in the letters and poems supposedly written during the period 1858–62 of a great emotional disturbance bordering on mental instability. Under one prevalent theory the separation caused by Bowles's trip to Europe was the apogee of Emily's building despair and led her to write Higginson. Although she has described in this diary (see No. 8) the emotional turning point at which she decided to seek Higginson's advice, it may well be that Bowles's departure—and perhaps with it all hope of "understanding – of love the shining symbol"— enhanced her desperate need to share her poetic gift with someone who might respond in a way Bowles could not.

The commencement tea to which Emily refers may have been the one that took place in the summer of 1860, and her poem 322, "There came a day at Summer's full" (1861), may describe the same experience recounted in this entry.

In her last letter to Bowles Emily wrote, "It is strange that the most intangible thing is the most adhesive."

For additional insight into the relationship, see Nos. 34, 51, and 70.

Euterpe in Greek mythology was the muse of music and lyric poetry.

(Letter 187, about 1858)

Dear Master

I am ill, but grieving more that you are ill, I make my stronger hand work long eno' to tell you. I thought perhaps you were in Heaven, and when you spoke again, it seemed quite sweet, and wonderful, and surprised me so – I wish that you were well.

I would that all I love, should be weak no more. The Violets are by my side, the Robin very near, and "Spring" – they say, Who is she – going by the door –

Indeed it is God's house – and these are gates of Heaven, and to and fro, the angels go, with their sweet postillions – I wish that I were great, like Mr. Michael Angelo, and could paint for you. You ask me what my flowers said – then they were disobedient – I gave them messages. They said what the lips in the West, say, when the sun goes down, and so says the Dawn.

Listen again, Master. I did not tell you that today had been the Sabbath Day.

Each Sabbath on the Sea, makes me count the Sabbaths, till we meet on shore – and (will the) whether the hills will look as blue as the sailors say. I cannot talk any more (stay any longer) tonight (now), for this pain denies me.

How strong when weak to recollect, and easy, quite, to love. Will you tell me, please to tell me, soon as you are well.

(Emily's alternate wording is in parentheses.)

(Letter 233, about 1861)

Master.

If you saw a bullet hit a Bird – and he told you he was'nt shot – you might weep at his courtesy, but you would certainly doubt his word.

One drop more from the gash that stains your Daisy's bosom – then would you *believe?* Thomas' faith in Anatomy, was stronger than his faith in faith. God made me – [Sir] Master – I did'nt be – myself. I dont know how it was done. He built the heart in me – Bye and bye it outgrew me – and like the little mother – with the big child – I got tired holding him. I heard of a thing called "Redemption" – which rested men and women. You remember I asked you for it – you gave me something else. . . .

I dont know what you can do for it – thank you – Master – but if I had the Beard on my cheek – like you – and you – had Daisy's petals – and you cared so for me – what would become of you? . . . What would you do with me if I came "in white?" Have you the little chest to put the Alive – in?

I want to see you more – Sir – than all I wish for in this world – and the wish – altered a little – will be my only one – for the skies.

. . . Would Daisy disappoint you – no – she would'nt – Sir – it were comfort forever – just to look in your face, while you looked in mine – then I could play in the woods till Dark – till you take me where Sundown cannot find us – and the true keep coming – till the town is full. . . .

I did'nt think to tell you, you did'nt come to me "in white," nor ever told me why,

> No Rose, yet felt myself a'bloom,
> No Bird – yet rode in Ether.

(The original letter is quite long and has been excerpted here. The bracketed word is one Emily crossed out.)

(Letter 248, about 1862)

Oh, did I offend it – [Did'nt it want me to tell it the truth] Daisy – Daisy – offend it – who bends her smaller life to his (it's) meeker (lower) every

64

day – who only asks – a task – [who] something to do for love of it – some little way she cannot guess to make that master glad –

A love so big it scares her, rushing among her small heart – pushing aside the blood and leaving her faint (all) and white in the gust's arm –

Daisy – who never flinched thro' that awful parting, but held her life so tight he should not see the wound – who would have sheltered him in her childish bosom (Heart) – only it was'nt big eno' for a Guest so large. . . .

Low at the knee that bore her once unto [royal] wordless rest [now] Daisy [stoops a] kneels a culprit – tell her her [offence] fault – Master – if it is [not so] small eno' to cancel with her life, [Daisy] she is satisfied – but punish [do not] dont banish her – shut her in prison, Sir – only pledge that you will forgive – sometime – before the grave, and Daisy will not mind – She will awake in [his] your likeness.

Wonder stings me more than the Bee – who never did sting me – but made gay music with his might wherever I [may] [should] did go – Wonder wastes my pound, you said I had no size to spare – . . .

Oh how the sailor strains, when his boat is filling – Oh how the dying tug, till the angel comes. Master – open your life wide, and take me in forever, I will never be tired – I will never be noisy when you want to be still. I will be [glad] [as the] your best little girl – nobody else will see me, but you – but that is enough – I shall not want any more – and all that Heaven only will disappoint me – will be because it's not so dear

(The letter is excerpted. Bracketed words are Emily's deletions; words in parentheses are alternates.)

(322)

There came a Day at Summer's full,
Entirely for me –
I thought that such were for the Saints,
Where Resurrections – be –

The Sun, as common, went abroad,
The flowers, accustomed, blew,
As if no soul the solstice passed
That maketh all things new –

The time was scarce profaned, by speech –
The symbol of a word
Was needless, as at Sacrament,
The Wardrobe – of our Lord –

Each was to each The Sealed Church,
Permitted to commune this – time –
Lest we too awkward show
At Supper of the Lamb.

The Hours slid fast – as Hours will,
Clutched tight, by greedy hands –
So faces on two Decks, look back,
Bound to opposing lands –

And so when all the time had leaked,
Without external sound
Each bound the Other's Crucifix –
We gave no other Bond –

Sufficient troth, that we shall rise –
Deposed – at length, the Grave –
To that new Marriage,
Justified – through Calvaries of Love –

The day I flew too close to Bliss –
The brilliance of the glow
Reflected by Eternity
Inflamed my feathered soul –

The passion known to Icarus
Infused my hour of flight –
Until Truth's melting – when I fell
Restrainless – from the light!

[27]

Monday, June 3

A warming breeze has called me from the house –
and I escape to nature's blue-walled writing chamber
– grass for my chair, a pencil for companion. Father
is at the office, Mother asleep, and Vinnie sewing

fiercely – so none but the bee – interrupted at dinner
– will know how I neglect the household for these
few quiet moments. If he disapproves my truantship,
he keeps his own counsel.

June deafens us with splendor. The flowers make
an orchestra of purple, orange, and red, and the sky
trumpets it's brilliance. Now we feel a promise long
withheld by penurious Winter. Hope perches in the
heart and beats it's wings against our funeral
thoughts. I have a Summer soul – that sings more
freely in her warmth.

The image in the second paragraph recalls poem 254, "'Hope' is the thing with feathers –" (1861).

> (254)
> "Hope" is the thing with feathers –
> That perches in the soul –
> And sings the tune without the words –
> And never stops – at all –
>
> And sweetest – in the Gale – is heard –
> And sore must be the storm –
> That could abash the little Bird
> That kept so many warm –

I've heard it in the chillest land –
And on the strangest Sea –
Yet, never, in Extremity,
It asked a crumb – of Me.

To doubt that Daisies plan return
And Roses find their place
Once more against the stony wall –
Were the defeat of Bliss –
To witness Summer's face withdraw –
And leaves reduce their stay –
Say more of loss than countless souls
Swept to Eternity.

[28]

Thursday, June 6

The Book Notice of the Express describes a book just
published with the title "Our Eternal Homes." The
author – a "Bible student" – discusses such topics as
"What Is Heaven?" "Heavenly Scenery" and "Death
the Gate of Life." The notice says the book "furnishes

much food for thought and does not attempt to draw conclusions that are not plainly involved in the suggestive words of the holy writ."

I should like to read a book whose author holds the key to those unfathomable mysteries! Does he truly comprehend the plain suggestions of the holy writ? The Bible always left me reeling with questions. When Father reads us a passage, I know he wishes us to aim our thoughts in it's direction, but mine more often follow a meandering course. He reads of "Heaven" and I think of a June day ablaze in it's own glory. Will there be such days in that far tomorrow? It must be a lovely place that detains it's visitors so long. Heaven is our last surprise.

When the Bible proclaims eternal life, I hear only the silent drop of Death. Does Life color our days with anguish to lessen our affection for Mortality?

That majestic Book and I have long been acquaintances – I wish we might be better <u>friends</u>.

The Book Notice column of the *Express* for June 6, 1867, announced the arrival of this book, describing it as "a sort of familiar study of the Bible to get all the facts that are revealed on these points."

Lower than angels –
We refrain
To approach
Their vaunted plane –
Fearful lest
The promised Crown
Were a dimmer
Than our own

[29]

Tuesday, June 11

Austin and Father retreated from their office
together this evening and Austin stopped for supper
with us. A political discussion ensued – leading as it
often does to the verge of a quarrel before amity was
restored. That is the strange but usual conclusion. I
often wonder how their partnership can thrive when
they are so disparate in temperament, joined by
scarcely more than blood. It has always been so, since
Austin was old enough to form opinions. He and
Father grip conviction so firmly that conflict is the

inevitable result! But it is finally superficial. Each has always idolized the other – though it somewhat dismays Father that Austin is not his duplicate!

After the clearing up, Austin and I chatted in the kitchen while Father repaired to his study and Mother and Vinnie shared the Republican in the parlor. I showed him my latest verse and he expressed polite approval. He encourages me to write – but I suspect it is only because he thinks the occupation suitable for an unmarried sister. If he sees beyond he never says.

Emily was always close to her older brother, Austin, as is particularly evident from her affectionate letters to him written while he was away from home teaching in Boston and later attending Harvard Law School. After graduating from Harvard in 1854, he went into partnership with his father and continued to practice law in Amherst for the rest of his life.

In one of these early letters Emily commented, "I do think it's so funny – you and father do nothing but 'fisticuff' all the while you're at home, and the minute you are separated, you become such devoted friends; but this is a checkered life."

For more on Austin, see Nos. 71, 85, and 92.

Friday, June 14

Sometimes Vinnie's power to persuade overcomes my
own to refuse. Father's stubbornness resides in us
both. Two opposing trains on the same track must
halt or come to grief – unless one find a branching
route. Today she conquered – and I went with her to
Adams to overlook their newest wares. She longs for
new curtains for her bedroom and is seeking a
suitable fabric. In the shop I tried to make myself
invisible but could not escape the eager eye of old
Mrs. Alice Dickinson (from another house). To avoid
her overbearing presence I pretended not to see her.
But soon I heard her rasping voice emerge from a
bolt of cloth. The cloth spoke to a companion. "There
is Edward Dickinson's daughter Lavinia – and can
that be her sister Emily with her? 'Twould be most
surprising – she is rarely seen about. Have you met
her? No? I knew her in her youth. She has been
strange from girlhood – some say mad – and finds
society beneath her notice."

What a sharp summary – delivered slyly behind
silk! The lady may have fancied herself hidden from

our ears – but her words seemed too loud for chance!
She only speaks the wider opinion – of those who
do not know that madness may be wisdom in divine
disguise. A spot of madness undresses a mind too
tightly garbed. Each person sees the world at his
own angle.

Our efforts to acquire went unrewarded –
Vinnie found nothing to her taste – and I regretted
the excursion.

Emily's reputation as an eccentric, fairly well established by this time, increased as she became more reclusive.

The language in the second paragraph calls to mind poem 435, "Much Madness is divinest Sense" (1862).

See also the note to No. 39.

J. S. & C. Adams was an Amherst store that carried a variety of goods.

There were many unrelated Dickinson families in Amherst, as a trek through the town's cemetery will attest.

(435)

Much Madness is divinest Sense –
To a discerning Eye –
Much Sense – the starkest Madness –
'Tis the Majority
In this, as All, prevail –

Assent – and you are sane –
Demur – you're straightway dangerous –
And handled with a Chain –

[31]

Wednesday, June 19

Today was Ned's sixth birthday. Sue invited several
local children for a party this afternoon. I can hear
their shouts from my window – the carefree cries of
youth still unanointed by grief.

It seems but yesterday that my nephew arrived
among us – and suddenly one became two, enlarging
our small world. Sue found a new companion, who
demands more than many. Poor Austin I think is
still perplexed by fatherhood.

Ned has grown so fast. I remember when he first
gained the mastery of his legs. How proud a day
when those disobedient feet were conquered and he
stepped – alone – into the future. His shining eyes
announced his independence from the guiding hand.
Just so a completed soul discards it's props and learns
to stand alone. It needs no one beyond to make a self.

For a similar use of the "props" imagery, refer to poem 1142, "The Props assist the House" (1863).

(1142)

The Props assist the House
Until the House is built
And then the Props withdraw
And adequate, erect,
The House support itself
And cease to recollect
The Auger and the Carpenter –
Just such a retrospect
Hath the perfected Life –
A past of Plank and Nail
And slowness – then the Scaffolds drop
Affirming it a Soul.

 [32]

Saturday, June 22

This morning I crossed the hedge to return Sue's Nicholas Nickleby. While I was there, an elderly acquaintance came to call – and was at the door before I had a chance to flee. Sue said, "Emily and I were just discussing Dickens" to which the formi-

dable matron replied, "I do not care for the man myself – nor for reading generally" – her tone a mixture of condescension and sympathy that we should abuse our time in such a fashion! She then chattered on irrepressibly about local happenings. I scarcely listened to the chronicle and eyed the front door longingly but feared to show discourtesy in Sue's home. Finally the woman's voice seemed to fail her, and with a croak she took her leave – "with which we willingly parted," whereupon we wicked two surrendered to our mirth!

In reward for my long endurance, Sue again lent me Thomas a Kempis. It is a volume we exchange often – for it's wisdom must be tasted slowly like the richest food. I look forward to every day that brings a new book – or renewal of acquaintance with an old. Reading is the resonance of ideas on the Soul's willing ear. It is a lonely mind through which the thoughts of another have not passed.

The Dickinson family library at Harvard contains books from the households of both the Homestead and the Evergreens. The families' books have been mixed, and it is generally not possible to determine when or by whom they were acquired. There is a copy of *Nicholas Nickleby* in that collection, though Emily is not known to have referred to the book in any writing other than this diary entry. Whether the particular copy mentioned here and the one in the collection are the same cannot be known for certain.

Sue owned the 1857 edition of the fifteenth-century work *Of the Imitation of Christ* by Thomas à Kempis, which—as has long been assumed and is now confirmed by this entry—she shared with Emily. Her copy contains markings that may have been made by both women. As a Christmas present in 1876, Sue gave Emily a copy of the new edition that had been published that year.

The quotation in the first paragraph is probably a reference to Hamlet's reply to Polonius in *Hamlet,* act 2, scene 2.

 [33]

Tuesday, June 25

The night is so clear I can see the stars from my window. In a murky hour Faith is all that holds them there – but now we have the proof of their existence. On such a night Death seems distant – but we know it deceives. We have too little time to let the dimmest star escape our notice. When they go out, we wait for brighter evenings. To live – and look upon their splendor – costs us much in anguish. I never knew a

Bliss without. Yet we willingly pay the price – since
Doubt deprives us of farther vision.

[34]

Saturday, June 29

Mr. Bowles arrived last night and stays with Austin
and Sue. He stopped here this afternoon to take tea
with us. I felt a fright at first and would have fled
from the parlor – but he was there before I heard his
step. Vinnie and Mother gave immediate welcome. I
believe Mother – well today – would rise with little
effort from a sick bed to see him, so much do his
stories delight her.

His visits still bring joy to all – though mine is
tempered by remembrance. Those triumphant eyes
brighten our door. They are beacons of a lively mind
– though cleverness may substitute for understanding. Before leaving he thanked me for the "puzzle" I
enclosed with my last letter to him. He always finds
my Snow inscrutable. He sees "through a dark glass"
like Mr. Higginson and Dr. Holland. My words
race beyond them and they think the chase fruitless.

Riddle is not my aim – beyond what Life itself poses. But one must not come to a poem safely – as to the doorstep of a friend who has a warm supper waiting. A word anticipated never singed the Soul. Sudden fire is divine peril – and begins and ends in Bliss.

This entry reemphasizes Emily's frustration at Bowles's inability to appreciate her art. But in spite of the mental and spiritual gulf that always existed between them, she continued to hold Bowles in high regard until his death in 1878. In one of her last letters to him, written in 1877, she again used the adjective "triumphant" to describe his appearance: "You have the most triumphant Face out of Paradise. . . ."

Emily's description of her initial reluctance to greet Bowles is reminiscent of her reaction to one of his earlier visits, when she sent down a note saying she could not see him. She later wrote to explain that she had given up her time with him so that Austin and Vinnie could have more.

In her letters to Bowles Emily sometimes referred to her verses as "Snow." Unfortunately, this entry gives no clue to the identity of the poem he found so "puzzling" here.

Dr. Josiah Holland was an associate of Samuel Bowles at the *Republican* when this entry was written. He founded *Scribner's Monthly* in 1870. His wife, Elizabeth, was one of Emily's closest friends and principal correspondents. For more on the Hollands, see Nos. 37, 62, 88, and 95.

The dark glass is presumably an allusion to the famous passage from I Corinthians 13:12.

[35]

Monday, July 1

I have finished a letter to Peter tonight, enclosing
this verse. It may please him to know I too can
speak of divinity though unschooled in the doctrines
that mold his days.

My verses are my richest gifts – because they
carry love exceeding plainer words. I have been
abstemious lest any suppose that superfluity
whelms Value. But do I presume above myself?
Do the recipients merely smile and set the lines
aside, indulging whimsey? Comment is rare –
unless I seek special counsel – as from Mr. Higginson or on occasion Sue. Yet still I spread my failed
flowers – never knowing if the pods be colorful to
other eyes. Their hues please _me_. Perhaps I share
Narcissus' motive!

Perez Dickinson Cowan was a favorite cousin of Emily's whom she
always referred to as "Peter." He graduated from Amherst College in
1866 and later attended Union Theological Seminary, where he was
apparently studying at the time this entry was written. He was ordained

a Presbyterian minister in 1869 and served churches in Tennessee, New York, and New Jersey.

The allusion in the second paragraph is to Emily's poem 404, "How many Flowers fail in Wood" (1862).

(404)

How many Flowers fail in Wood –
Or perish from the Hill –
Without the privilege to know
That they are Beautiful –

How many cast a nameless Pod
Upon the nearest Breeze –
Unconscious of the Scarlet Freight –
It bear to Other Eyes –

The ark of Faith is wide enough
To welcome Doubters in
Who test the weight of airy planks
Uncertified of men –

Probing the wood's resilience
Against the deadly gale –
What Captain minds the Compass
That guides the timid Sail –

Then – trusting in a buoyant Truth –
They – halting – file aboard
And never to the shore look back
From whence the Ship is steered –

[36]

Thursday, July 4

The house is mine this afternoon. Mother, Father, and Vinnie have gone to a July Fourth picnic at the Guertises. I decline all such invitations, but Vinnie went willingly. She expects to find enjoyment in

random association – but I prefer to choose my own
moments of communion.

Corporeal presence does not relieve loneliness if
understanding be absent. Though "two are gathered
together" fellowship may fail. It is supremest comfort
to be content with one's own society. That inner
friend is our acutest listener.

The *Hampshire Express* for July 4, 1867, noted that a picnic to celebrate
the day would be held under the trees in front of the residence of Mr.
John Guertis.

The quotation is probably from Matthew 18:20.

The finest Habitation
Is inner than the Walls
Supporting Architecture –
Where Ordinary dwells.

Though it surpasses – Structure –
It has the shape of Home –
Where Thought and Soul – Companions –
Share a solitary room.

It's Window is a mirror,
It's door defy the key –
No gate secure it's garden –
Except Eternity.

 [37]

Saturday, July 6

I am felonious – my crime neglect of Mrs. Holland's
latest letter. I was guilty once before – and felt a
shame when her words lay so long unanswered and
lonely on the desk. But then it was too hard to tame
my thoughts for any page but Poetry. In those years
it filled all hollow corners. Now I cross that bound-
ary with looser feet. She is my second sister – who
holds me in affection like the first but attends more
closely! I share my heart with her more often than
most – but not enough to tire her charity. She even
has the color of a parent. I put before her thoughts
I dare not lay in Mothers path – for <u>she</u> astounds
too easily.

When I send Mrs. Holland a sorrow she returns
it to me mended. For illness of the body she always

knows a remedy. Yet merriment is her finest
gown – and so I gather up delights like fabric scraps
and weave her patterns from the days. These gifts
she seems to treasure – The others incite no comment. I guess my verses dont brighten her wardrobe!
I wonder if she keeps them in a drawer with other
purgatory pieces – the unworn things that live
between the world and final resting. My finest Art
she overlooks but perhaps she sees a letter's shape
more clearly. Tonight I'll show her – the humming-
bird that danced with a bee and set the bush aflame
– while our children played with elves in the garden
– My blanket scarleted the grass and made us all a
nest – which was more blissful than ornithology!
These are the majesty of living.

Emily's friendship with Dr. Josiah Holland and his wife, Elizabeth, began in the 1850s and continued until her death. Ninety-four of her letters to them have been found. Emily and Vinnie visited the couple on at least two occasions in the early years, and the Hollands made occasional visits to Amherst. Mrs. Holland particularly was one of Emily's closest confidantes. From 1865 on, the letters were addressed almost exclusively to her.

In one letter she suggested, "Perhaps you laugh at me! Perhaps the whole United States are laughing at me too! *I* can't stop for that! *My* business is to love. I found a bird . . . on a little bush at the foot of the garden, and wherefore sing, I said, since nobody *hears?*

"One sob in the throat . . . '*My* business is to *sing'* – and away she rose!"

The passage presumably sums up Emily's own view of her poetic mission, but, as Emily herself suggests in this entry, there is no indication that her artistry had much of an impact on the Hollands, even though she sent them thirty-one of her poems.

On another occasion she wrote, "The Wind blows gay today and the Jays bark like Blue Terriers. . . . I hold you few I love, till my heart is red as Febuary and purple as March." Elsewhere, displaying her famous facility for aphorism, she observed, "After you went, a low wind warbled through the house like a spacious bird, making it high but lonely. . . . The supper of the heart is when the guest has gone." Showing the side of her nature that regarded life, despite its inherent sorrow, as a glorious experience, she remarked in 1870, "Life is the finest secret."

The fanciful metaphoric language used in her letters to Mrs. Holland is typical of that found throughout much of her correspondence, as well as in the diary. (It is often obscure, and one suspects that the recipients must occasionally have been mystified.) This entry provides a representative example of the style.

There is a three-year hiatus (1862–65) in the correspondence between Emily and the Hollands. The most obvious assumption is that these letters were lost, but it has also been suggested that Mrs. Holland deliberately destroyed the ones she received in order to conceal some secret about Emily's life and loves. An explanation for at least part of the gap is provided by Emily's confession in the first paragraph of this entry.

The blanket mentioned in the second paragraph presumably refers to the red blanket with black stripes that, according to her niece, Emily used to spread on the ground to sit on. Visitors to the Homestead can see it in Emily's bedroom.

For more on the Hollands, see Nos. 62, 88, and 95.

 [38]

Wednesday, July 10

It was a busy day. Vinnie and I bustled all morning with preparations for the Commencement tea, assisted by Fanny and Loo. They arrived last night for the occasion, which would falter without their obliging graces. Having no regular help, we called in Mrs. Bates to assist with serving. Mother, feeling better after a week of lethargy, oversaw the whole. Father supervised the placement of tables and chairs on the lawn by Mr. Church and Pat. The grass was still wet from last night's storm, but the sun and breeze had drained all the dew by this afternoon. The rain cleared the air wonderfully, and July's heat was cooled by unaccustomed balms. Nature is in it's fullest glory and has seldom been more accommodating for our annual event.

Guests began to arrive by four, though our "official hour" was six. Vinnie and I served conversation with the sandwiches. To chirp inconsequentials gives Vinnie no discomfort but for me is now more painful than formerly. Preferring flight, I nonetheless – for Fathers sake – did my part. Later I retreated to the dining room to pour sherry for those who sought it. There I was revived by the company and conversation of Judge and Mrs. Lord, who are at Amherst House for several days. They never miss our teas – which would be much the poorer without them!

The day retired before the guests. A few still lingered in the dwindling light. Father seemed unwilling for the last to go. I believe this is his favorite day of the year. The occasion is august – as befits his participation – but levity is not untoward. He *can therefore permit himself a crumb or two! He pronounced today a great success – and none were heard to disagree.*

Commencement at Amherst College was one of the social highlights of the year for the small community. The various events occupied most of the week. Of particular importance was the annual tea held at the home of Edward Dickinson on Wednesday of Commencement Week. The *Express* for July 11, 1867, reported that the weather had been more favorable than usual for all the Commencement exercises.

Horace Church was responsible for looking after the grounds of the Homestead and was employed by the Dickinsons from at least the 1850s until his death in 1881. "Pat," not otherwise identified, was mentioned several times in Emily's letters and appears to have been a groomsman or general handyman. This is the only known reference to Mrs. Bates.

Frequent visitors to the Commencement tea and to the Dickinson home on other occasions were Judge and Mrs. Otis Phillips Lord, who lived in Salem. Judge Lord was a close friend of Edward Dickinson, whom he may have met during the 1850s when they were both actively involved in Whig politics.

For more on Emily's relationship with Judge Lord, see Nos. 61, 65, 69, 77, 86, 90, and 100.

For a note on Fanny and Loo, see No. 4.

Friday, July 12

A word from Mr. Higginson saved the day from
commonness. He finds my latest efforts to his liking
– and I rejoice in the victory! I always hope to make
a verse that pleases him – to repay his patient listen-
ing – but the lines so often gallop off when he would
have me rein them. Why then does he not abandon
so disobedient a follower? Does he think me worthy
of his mighty efforts – or am I only Curiosity? I am
not bold enough to ask – though the question dogs
me. Others look astonished when I speak – I hoped
that he would understand. I fear I cant be reshaped
– but God takes pity on his Kangaroo.

The student of Dickinson might well ask the same question that Emily does here, since the reason for the attraction between Higginson and his pupil is no clearer from his perspective than from hers. As we have seen, he advised her against publication and had no real appreciation of her work until after her death. In the October 1891 issue of the *Atlantic* he gave his own assessment of the relationship, finding "on my side an interest that was strong and even affectionate, but not based on any thorough comprehension; and on her side a hope, always rather baffled, that I should afford some aid in solving her abstruse problem of life."

Emily was no doubt right, however, in assuming that he also regarded her as something of a curiosity. After his first visit with her, he wrote his wife, "I never was with any one who drained my nerve power so much. . . . I am glad not to live near her." In later years he described her as "my partially cracked Poetess at Amherst."

For her part Emily was always aware of her position as an outsider. As she told Higginson, "All men say 'What' to me, but I thought it a fashion – ." Elsewhere she observed to him, "Perhaps you smile at me. I could not stop for that – My Business is Circumference – An ignorance, not of Customs, but if caught with the Dawn – or the Sunset see me – Myself the only Kangaroo among the Beauty, Sir, if you please, it afflicts me, and I thought that instruction would take it away." (See also No. 30.)

Regardless of whatever more complicated motives may have been involved, perhaps the most definable basis for the relationship was simply a mutual respect and affection developed through their correspondence, as well as a tenacious conviction that, though they were so often at cross-purposes, each had something to offer the other.

 [40]

Wednesday, July 17

The days and nights have been sultry this past week. Scarcely a breath comes through my bedroom window. I am sorry for Father as he trudges back to his office after dinner. He is always garbed so properly, summer and winter, from top hat to walking cane.

He spares himself nothing in propriety just to accommodate Nature. For accommodation is not in the nature of Father!

At dinner he related to us some details of an extraordinary will contest in which he is now involved. So avaricious are the competing relatives that it appears the testator's will may not be done. How confounding is the Law. Justice puts out her sign so that all men might find her – yet when they call she is so often not at home!

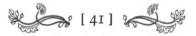 [41]

Tuesday, July 23

Ned and Clara paid a visit this afternoon while I tended my flowers. Their interruption delights as few others do. The sky glowed like lazuli and the breeze was full of balms. My little nephew looks for any opportunity to cross the hedge. I guess he finds his aunts sufficient substitutes for sprightlier companions, of which he has'nt many. His sister is still too new to appreciate the world – and parental attentions are meager during the day.

While Ned ran through the garden in search of bees, Clara and I talked, as is our custom and special joy. He is fortunate to be in her care. She has been more encumbered by troubles than a girl should be, but still her compassionate nature goes beyond patience. I have watched her grow strong and straight and am confident she will shape her future to a happier mold, for she has the passion to see how mighty life can be.

Now she trembles when she thinks of the Future – but do not all God's creatures? Ability gives her choice – despite the world's circumscriptions – but, like most young women, she sees only one path to happiness. At the age of twenty-three she thinks herself old and fears she may never find her life's companion. As Austin's house was never hers, she seeks a separate household of her own devising.

I guess she thinks it strange I never sought the same. Perhaps she does'nt suspect that I once shared the dreams of every girl – until a larger dream surpassed them. Then I saw that the freedom – to sing – was as great as love. If "wife" were now my title – could I be midwife? What profit to "gain a household and lose a soul"? A captured bird mutes it's tune.

But Clara must answer to her own soul. I advise her to be patient. Deferred dreams are more startling in fulfillment.

The minutes passed unnoticed – until they made an hour. Ned protested Clara's summons as usual but was calmed by the promise of return in a few days. The wily child again "forgot" to fetch home all he had brought. This time he left a wooden toy cart beneath the cherry tree. The imp knows his doting aunt will not return it empty! Thus Fate decrees tomorrow a day for gingerbread!

For a brief biography of Clara Newman, see the note to No. 13. According to an account by Clara's niece, Clara and Anna were mistreated by Sue while they lived at the Evergreens. Clara married Sidney Turner of Norwich, Connecticut, in 1869.

In her own reminiscences of Emily Dickinson, Clara related that she often engaged in private conversations with Emily, who would always listen sympathetically and offer encouragement. Even after her marriage, when Clara would occasionally return for a brief stay at the house, she looked forward to visiting alone with Emily in her room late in the evening. Clara's account of Ned's leaving his things at the Homestead is corroborated by this entry.

The allusion in the fourth paragraph seems to be a paraphrase of Mark 8:36.

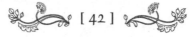 [42]

Saturday, July 27

Libbie and Mr. Currier stayed a night with us
and departed this morning. They are a confounding
couple. Their recent union appears harmonious –
but Libbie always seemed more comfortable with
dissonance. I never thought that she would yield
to capture!

She has been with us often since our youth and
yet to me she is still a daunting figure. She fascinates
and overwhelms. Breath taken when she enters is not
expelled until she leaves. I wonder Mr. Currier – a
temperate gentleman – dared approach her with his
bold proposal. Perhaps the suggestion was hers. She
seemed independent as a bird, but I guess she tired of
solitary flight!

Elizabeth Dickinson Currier, whom Emily sometimes called "Aunt Libbie" or "Libbie," was Edward Dickinson's youngest sister, only seven years older than Emily. She appears, from the descriptions in Emily's letters, to have been a rather formidable lady. Her niece once referred to her as "the only male relative on the female side."

Elizabeth Dickinson married Augustus Currier in October 1866, at the age of forty-three.

[43]

Monday, July 29

It is ten o'clock and the evening is silent except for Summer's murmuring creatures. Father is in Springfield and Mother and Vinnie have gone to bed, Vinnie complaining of fatigue after an excess of dusting! This is the hour of my Soul's free floating – when I can give myself utterly to verse. The others think I "play at paste" – but none suspect how deep I dive for pearl. I wonder they do not occasionally ask what I have been about, alone in my room after the pies are baked and the mending finished. Is the palsy invisible to others? When I feel the impulse surge within me, the World is a distant place. Then I cannot stop for instants. I must push to completion or

perish by degrees. I have given all I have for the
pearl of greatest price. Payment has left me solitary
– but recompensed beyond imagination.

The quoted words are from poem 320, "We play at Paste" (1862). The biblical allusion in the next-to-last sentence is to Matthew 13:46.

In one letter Emily told Higginson, "And when . . . a sudden light on Orchards, or a new fashion in the wind troubled my attention – I felt a palsy, here – the Verses just relieve – ."

(320)

We play at Paste –
Till qualified, for Pearl –
Then, drop the Paste –
And deem ourself a fool –

The Shapes – though – were similar –
And our new Hands
Learned *Gem*-Tactics –
Practicing *Sands* –

Thursday, August 1

I brought the Express to my room tonight after the others had all seen it to peruse before sleep comes. My eye fell on the notice about the trial of John Surratt, now taking place in Washington. It has already consumed forty-five days. There is so much evidence against him that his fate seems inescapable.

Horror hides in every year. It surprises us most just when we think we shall pass in safety. We lost a president – then – but a friend may leave at any hour. The war laid it's hand on us all but the weight was unequally shared. Life is more democratic – No heart but felt her leaden grasp.

What I read of Mr. Lincoln made me feel the pain of his departure. But he had done his work – and therefore left no spoils for Death. To steal a life before it's close is unforgivable.

The world of presidents is far from mine – though I see it daily charted and never miss the observation. That wider orbit daunts my feet – I cant keep my balance. But a single thread joins mighty to meek. Death, Exhiliration and the

*Perfidies of the Universe make companions of
housewife and statesman.*

The content of this entry is unusual because in her letters Emily rarely commented on current events or expressed any political opinions, though she apparently read the newspapers with avid interest. In a letter of 1884 to Mrs. Holland she facetiously remarked, "'George Washington was the Father of his Country' – 'George Who?'"

"That sums all Politics to me – . . ."

The *Express* closely followed the trial of John H. Surratt, who was implicated in the conspiracy to assassinate Lincoln (he had escaped to Canada after the crime but was captured and returned for trial). The jury failed to agree on a verdict, and he was ultimately released.

 [45]

Monday, August 5

*This morning while rearranging my papers I found
Katie's last letter. I miss her voice and wonder why
she never answers mine. Affection is a slippery thing
and needs a stubborn grip. I thought our bond was
more adhesive. We seemed to have a match of minds
but that was mostly in Sue's parlor, where laughter*

lifts the vails. But – away from the drawing room –
I have'nt much of "world" in me. I always enjoyed
our quiet conversations but Kate is used to louder
thoughts. She has traveled much and wears a
burnish got from others. Perhaps my twinkle is too
pale for her.

　　Sue says she has become a "millionaire" again.
Does that restrain her from me?

　　I cling to all who touch my heart but even more
to those she draws inside. The first are many – the
second few. Departure diminishes those left behind.
I'll write to Katie and learn if her love be retrievable.

Catherine (Kate) Scott Turner Anthon was a friend of Susan Dickinson,
whom she had met when they both attended Utica Female Seminary as
girls. In 1859 she visited Sue in Amherst and became acquainted with
Emily. They apparently developed a warm friendship, as is suggested by
the five extant letters Emily sent her between 1859 and 1866. These com-
prise the only known correspondence between them, and the specific
date assigned to each letter is only conjectural.

　　These letters, as well as selected language from letters to other friends
and from the poems, formed the basis for the 1951 biography by Rebecca
Patterson, *The Riddle of Emily Dickinson* (Boston: Houghton Mifflin), in
which she posited a lesbian affair between Emily and Kate, ended when

Kate broke it off for some reason. In Patterson's view, most of Emily Dickinson's poetry was only a "barren substitute" for this lost love.

It is of course impossible to disprove the existence of such a relationship, given the large gaps in documentation for the details of Emily's life, but the evidence to support it is thin. The hypothesis is based largely on speculations about meetings between the two women that may or may not have taken place (there is no evidence either way) and on a creative reading of some of the poetry. Moreover, Patterson's book was published before either the Master letters or Emily's eventual romance with Judge Otis Phillips Lord (see No. 61) had come to light.

No. 45 seems to undercut the idea of a love affair with Kate Anthon. The entry is a simple expression of sorrow at the apparent loss of a valued friendship; there is nothing in its tone to suggest the pain of sexual rejection.

In 1866 Kate married her second husband, John Anthon. It is this event to which Emily presumably refers in the second paragraph. In one of the letters she wrote, "You did not tell me you had once been a 'Millionaire'"—apparently alluding to her previous ignorance of the fact that Kate had once been married. (After her first husband's death in 1857, she had resumed using her maiden name.)

That Kate was never a particularly good correspondent is hinted at in letters where Emily chides her friend for her long periods of silence ("You cease indeed to talk, which is a custom prevalent among things parted and torn . . . ").

Thursday, August 8

My afternoon was partly spent in the entertainment
of a few neighborhood children, who watching me
labor in the garden as they passed in the street
below, perhaps assumed a venture up the hill would
bring some reward – a few merry words or a slice of
cake! Children seem to find my company inviting.
Perhaps they take me for a larger peer – who will
conspire with them against those wiser in the ways
of the world. If we are fortunate, a child always
lingers at our center – reminding us that end is not
far from beginning. They dwell in Hope's kingdom –
it's unchained denizens.

My visitors told me they were seeking "adven-
tures" and when I asked what kind they said such as
Robinson Crusoe found. I wished them well in the
pursuit and cautioned them against the Amherst
seas! For sustenance to brave the perils, I advised ice
cream, which we made fresh this morning. The
chickens have been happy – and we have eggs in
abundance. I think the offer almost made them
abandon ship! I brought them each a dish – a most

complaisant "Friday" – and one for myself – and we sat on the grass and dipped our spoons while they planned their travels. Then they tramped away – leaving me much amused – and I dont doubt they'll find us a frequent port.

Accounts of various contemporaries indicate that Emily enjoyed a special relationship with children. As we have seen, she felt a great affection for her niece and nephew, and she is known to have remained accessible to children even as she withdrew from the world of adults. In one letter she wrote, "I know but little of Little Ones, but love them very softly – ."

[47]

Monday, August 12

It grows late – but I can still hear Father in the parlor conversing with men from the college. Last night was similar – as he received a delegation from the Agricultural Society to discuss plans for the Cattle Show. He has so many demands on his time – and he seems wearier than usual in these humid days.

Edward Dickinson is a name much revered in
the community – if not everywhere beloved. Father
is valued for his good works and praised in his
profession. Success has clothed him in her customary
garb. But he has worn discontent all his life – as
lesser men who never reached his hight. What other
wealth did he seek that so eluded him? Does he feel
too large for Amherst? Perhaps he himself has never
been certain.

Blood dictates much to his daughter. It's substance
I accept but not the total rule. My search is in a
narrower circumference but – within – I give my
heart a wider run.

Life engages all in Battle – but Father never
learned that there are yielding times.

Edward Dickinson, as this entry notes, was a well-known and productive member of the Amherst community, carrying on the tradition of public service begun by his father, Samuel Fowler Dickinson. A prominent lawyer, Edward also served as treasurer of Amherst College for thirty-seven years, was active in Whig politics, and served in the General Court of Massachusetts, the state senate, and the United States Congress. In 1861 he was offered but refused the chance to run for lieutenant governor of

Massachusetts. He was in Boston representing his district in the General Court when he died suddenly in June 1874.

Yet as Emily sensed—and biographers have subsequently noted—the fruits of his strenuous exertions on behalf of family, community, and the Dickinson name somehow failed to satisfy him. Emily once wrote to a friend, "Father says in fugitive moments when he forgets the barrister & lapses into the man, says that his life has been passed in a wilderness or on an island – of late he says on an island" (quoted in Richard B. Sewall, *The Lyman Letters*). Commenting once on his illness in a letter to her cousin Louise Norcross, she said, "You know he never played, and the straightest engine has its leaning hour" – words that recall the last line of this entry.

For the Cattle Show see No. 57.

 [48]

Wednesday, August 14

Thievery is afoot in the garden! Birds have beset the cherry trees – and carried off a large part of the treasure we assigned to pies. They do no more than Nature's bidding – but still one wishes for a scruple in their kingdom.

We shape nature with a garden. But if she dont approve the plan, she sends her flocks and earthy armies to alter it. She promises neither success nor failure – for all is one to her – and she is heedless of

our efforts. It is we who put ourselves at her center –
and praise ourselves for a perfect fruit. This summer,
as in others, she has been kind to my flowers –
which return my affection. Surrounded by such
beauty we forget the hidden savagery. Nature gives
– but may at any time withdraw.

Gardening was one of Emily's favorite activities, and she was quite suc-
cessful at it. Flower and plant imagery is abundant in her poems.
See also No. 89.

[49]

Thursday, August 15

Another letter came from Mr. Wadsworth. They are
jewels to me – and when he encloses one of his
sermons – as today – no diamond had more fire. He
is a Poet in his own way. How often our minds
paint the same pictures – though we now inhabit
different worlds.

Our friendship has brightened a dozen years. I
was still a girl – and ill formed – when he promised

to lead me. Then my heart exceeded it's bounds and
Faith – overwhelmed – forgot it's questions. Our
conversations were confined to pages – but I used to
dream of nights when – meeting – we would cease to
talk and let our hearts be lips. Those girlish fantasies
have faded – and Inquiry is strong again. He never
suspected it's infirmity.

We could have had no life together – for he had
his vocation – from God – who chose him for divine
service. I cannot follow Heaven by Mr. Wadsworth's
path – but only with the steps my Art commands.
This is my peculiar calling – as true as his – but is
the source the same?

My friend knows my reluctance – and is patient
with me. He says that we are all shipwrecked sailors
grasping for land in a vast sea. God is on the shore
– and all who would be saved must struggle toward
it. His words are powerful – for he himself knows
the force of those waves – which batter will at every
turn. But there is solace in mutual striving.

We have met only once – But our bond is not a
creature of proximity. It is the understanding of how
a soul is forged – by anguish and renunciation.

A number of Dickinson scholars have supposed a romantic attachment between Wadsworth and Emily that culminated in an emotional crisis for her about 1862, when he moved (with his wife and family) to Calvary Church in San Francisco. (He returned to Philadelphia in 1869.) Whether or not his move occasioned a "crisis" (a now doubtful theory in light of diary entry No. 8), this entry is the most suggestive evidence so far discovered that at some point in her life Emily regarded Wadsworth as more than a friend but that the sentiment was unrequited. The language in No. 49 also suggests that he was the subject of two famous poems, "Wild Nights – Wild Nights!" (249; 1861) and "I cannot live with You" (640; 1862). Austin Dickinson commented after Emily's death that she had been in love several times in her own way.

However, it appears from this entry that the chief force behind her friendship with Wadsworth was her quest for guidance in matters of faith. The "shipwrecked sailors" metaphor recalls imagery found in poem 201, "Two swimmers wrestled on the spar – " (1860).

(249)
Wild Nights – Wild Nights!
Were I with thee
Wild Nights should be
Our luxury!

Futile – the Winds –
To a Heart in port –
Done with the Compass –
Done with the Chart!

Rowing in Eden –
Ah, the Sea!

Might I but moor – Tonight –
In Thee!

(640)
I cannot live with You –
It would be Life –
And Life is over there –
Behind the Shelf

The Sexton keeps the Key to –
Putting up
Our Life – His Porcelain –
Like a Cup –

Discarded of the Housewife –
Quaint – or Broke –
A newer Sevres pleases –
Old Ones crack –

I could not die – with You –
For One must wait
To shut the Other's Gaze down –
You – could not –

And I – Could I stand by
And see You – freeze –
Without my Right of Frost –
Death's privilege?

Nor could I rise – with You –
Because Your Face

Would put out Jesus'
That New Grace

Glow plain – and foreign
On my homesick Eye –
Except that You than He
Shone closer by –

They'd judge Us – How –
For You – served Heaven – You know,
Or sought to –
I could not –

Because You saturated Sight –
And I had no more Eyes
For sordid excellence
As Paradise

And were You lost, I would be –
Though My Name
Rang loudest
On the Heavenly fame –

And were You – saved –
And I – condemned to be
Where You were not –
That self – were Hell to Me –

So We must meet apart –
You there – I – here –
With just the Door ajar

That Oceans are – and Prayer –
And that White Sustenance –
Despair –

(201)

Two swimmers wrestled on the spar –
Until the morning sun –
When One – turned smiling to the land –
Oh God! the Other One!

The stray ships – passing –
Spied a face –
Upon the waters borne –
With eyes in death – still begging raised –
And hands – beseeching – thrown!

 [50]

Saturday, August 17

The downpours of the past week continue, making us feel Biblical. Only the dauntless foliage – thriving in the moisture – reminds us we are still tethered to earth. The works of man are not so fortunate. The floods have damaged the railroad tracks and blocked roads in some areas. Summer is too fleeting to go sunless. The treachery of other seasons in her is less forgivable. But her rains are less cruel than Winter's. The torrents – ceasing at intervals – leave the air scented, and warmth escapes unharmed. It is such a moment I steal now while the curtain gently billows and the dripping eaves play a simple melody. The sky grows white and the afternoon has not abandoned hope. Salvation in a sunbeam!

The Earth delights in summer Rain –
As feverish Saharan plain
Cries for a dew –
When Thunder surges – leaves expand –
The grasses' eager throats extend
To drink anew.

A gentle drop essays the air
To seek the cloud's assent before
It frees the Flood –
The torrent comes – and flowers vie
In fear and joy to satisfy
Each thirsting bud.

Then – when the World is washed, a peace
Almost surpassing holiness
Defines our Noon –
And in that soft, transporting hour
The garden glories in it's pow'r
To live again.

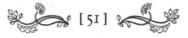 [51]

Saturday, August 24

Maria Whitney took tea with us this afternoon
after spending the night at the Evergreens. Escaping
Springfield, she finds a respit here, where she is
always welcome. We all wish her visits were more
frequent. Her conversation never palls nor makes me
wish to be elsewhere!

At present she is much occupied as general
caretaker of the Bowles household while Mrs.
Bowles' constitution trembles in anticipation of
another child. I suspect the arrangement is not
altogether a happy one. Mary is often difficult. That
Maria feels herself of use to the family – and

therefore bound to persevere – I have no doubt. But when I hear her speak – in the tenderest terms – of Mr. Bowles, I know her devotion exceeds Duty. Does she now feel as I felt – until my Heart lost it's battle with Imagination?

At our parting today, I saw a sorrowful reluctance in her eyes. Conscience – like a prickly household – does not yield easily to governance.

Maria Whitney, a distant relative of Samuel Bowles's wife, lived in Northampton but was a frequent visitor to the Bowles home in Springfield and often traveled with the family. From 1875 to 1880 she taught French and German at Smith College. In July of 1867 she moved into the Springfield house to help out while Mary Bowles was coping with one of her many pregnancies. The stay there was difficult, particularly after Maria learned from others that Mary was suspicious of her relationship with Mr. Bowles. Maria and Bowles were close, but there is no firm evidence that they were ever more than friends (though Emily appears to have suspected as much).

Maria also became friendly with the Dickinsons during the sixties. Though Emily's first known letter to her is tentatively dated 1877, it is now clear that their acquaintance had begun before that. In a letter to her sister-in-law, Lizzie, in late August 1867, Maria wrote that she had spent a pleasant day and a half in Amherst and that she would arrange for Lizzie to meet the Dickinsons the next year.

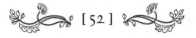

Friday, August 30

Today the stage brought the boxes Vinnie had
ordered from Boston. Among them was some new
pale green fabric for her. She could scarcely contain
her excitement at the thought of the dress she will
create. The pattern is elaborate – I dont know where
she will wear such a garment. We shall have a
dressmaker tomorrow to assist with the cutting. I
will help Vinnie with the sewing.

I myself am growing fond of white. It spares me
the choice and seems to suit me. I think I may soon
abandon other shades. To go in white – makes me
think of the pure page that awaits the verse. It is the
hue of victory – worn by the "ones who overcome."
A white dress is simplicity – like life "reduced to its
lowest terms."

It is not known exactly when Emily Dickinson decided to dress exclusively in white, but this entry gives some clues to her motivations. The
first quotation paraphrases Revelation 3:5. The second is from Thoreau's
Walden.

Monday, September 2

At supper tonight Father was in particularly
buoyant spirits and asked us each for details of the
day. I confined myself to the tasks my hands per-
formed – which never went beyond the ordinary –
and did not mention that my brain had wildly
celebrated six new lines! Mother met with several
friends this afternoon – and told us endless news of
all their children. Vinnie recounted her latest victory
– cloth for curtains is acquired – production has
begun! Father nodded – and occasionally remarked –
throughout our lengthy discourse.

It is not always plain – but I think he wants to
be a part of all our hours – to know that we are
happily engaged in life. He believes – to leave a
shred of self unused is tragedy. I never thought it
strictly true – what I said to Mr. Higginson – that
Father takes no time to notice what we do. The voice
that spoke those words was half creation – and
cannot vouch today for every fact.

The duties of a parent are to Father as weighty
as the lawyer's – But he seems a stranger to the
thought – that obligation has it's companion joy.

In her second letter to Higginson Emily described her parents in rather uncomplimentary terms: "My Mother does not care for thought – and Father, too busy with his Briefs – to notice what we do – ." It has been suggested that a number of the things she said to Higginson in these early letters cannot be taken completely seriously, particularly in light of seemingly conflicting comments elsewhere in her writing. In this entry Emily appears to admit as much.

[54]

Saturday, September 7

This morning from the kitchen I watched the squirrels leap fearlessly from branch to branch. How firm their spry sure-footed faith! And the birds on confident wings dived happily for feasts. Gods lower

creatures never fear a step amiss – nor ever lie abed
in hesitancy of the day. Our faith lacks such certi-
tude – but even weak it gives a comfort. It's absence
is Abyss too fathomless for thought.

I lost my footing once and tumbled in. In girlhood they told me God resided everywhere – and
I believed but could'nt feel Him watching. Later I
saw friends rush eagerly to His embrace but I –
slow to follow – was left behind. Then I took Poetry
for my master without a thought for His approval.
That power – beyond me to control – consumed my
soul – One day I had a question – and looked for
God to answer but he was nowhere to be found.
I was accustomed to the silence but believed it hid
a presence – revealed upon a summons. Now Being
was blank and had the taste of death. Faith may
come in many colors – but without – the world
is hueless.

Time and guidance from my friend restored.
I learned to walk again – with feet unsteady. But
still I test no branch without a thought for what
lies below!

If Emily Dickinson did experience a period of mental turmoil in the early sixties, perhaps another reason for it—in addition to the "terror" that her poetry was "numb" (see No. 8)—was the loss of faith described here. This entry is reminiscent of two poems assigned to the year 1862, "To lose one's faith – surpass" (377) and "I saw no Way – The Heavens were stitched – " (378).

There may also be a clue here to the significance of a more famous poem, "I felt a Funeral, in my Brain" (280; 1861), supposed by some to describe a mental breakdown.

Comments elsewhere in the diary suggest that the "friend" mentioned in the last paragraph may have been Charles Wadsworth (see Nos. 6 and 49). The only known letter from Wadsworth to Emily is undated but may have been written during the time in which this spiritual crisis took place. The letter begins, "I am distressed beyond measure at your note, . . . I can only imagine the affliction which has befallen, or is now befalling you." Wadsworth offers his sympathy and asks to learn "more definitely of your trial."

(377)
To lose one's faith – surpass
The loss of an Estate –
Because Estates can be
Replenished – faith cannot –

Inherited with Life –
Belief – but once – can be –
Annihilate a single clause –
And Being's – Beggary –

(378)

I saw no Way – The Heavens were stitched –
I felt the Columns close –
The Earth reversed her Hemispheres –
I touched the Universe –

And back it slid – and I alone –
A Speck upon a Ball –
Went out upon Circumference –
Beyond the Dip of Bell –

(280)

I felt a Funeral, in my Brain,
And Mourners to and fro
Kept treading – treading – till it seemed
That Sense was breaking through –

And when they all were seated,
A Service, like a Drum –
Kept beating – beating – till I thought
My Mind was going numb –

And then I heard them lift a Box
And creak across my Soul
With those same Boots of Lead, again,
Then Space – began to toll,

As all the Heavens were a Bell,
And Being, but an Ear,

And I, and Silence, some strange Race
Wrecked, solitary, here –

And then a Plank in Reason, broke,
And I dropped down, and down –
And hit a World, at every plunge,
And Finished knowing – then –

 [55]

Saturday, September 14

Mr. Bowles was with us since Thursday and
departed this morning for Boston and thence by
steamer to London. I wonder he has the will to travel
abroad so often when his strength and health flag
from constant motion – and the effort of his days.
Doubtless his mind and character are broadened by
these wider journeys. There are those for whom the
Transport of the body surpasses the Soul's.

I read nightly in the Republican of events far
beyond our door – from strange and wonderful
places no Dickinson will ever see. But such enjoyment as I have from these accounts satisfies all
thoughts of roaming. When I hear Father's train

whistle in the distance, I know it is bringing us the
world. I like the sound because it joins us with the
Vast. Hearing it from home – I need not go beyond.
I have "traveled much in Concord"!

Samuel Bowles traveled widely, despite frequent bouts of ill health, a subject of concern in a number of Emily's letters to him. His death in 1878 at the age of fifty-one was attributed to overwork.

One of Edward Dickinson's many accomplishments was his role in getting a railroad spur extended into Amherst. In 1851 the General Court granted a charter to the Amherst & Belchertown Rail Road, and in 1852 Edward became a director of the company.

The quotation in the last sentence is from Thoreau's *Walden*. A distant cousin of Emily's claimed that Thoreau was one of her favorite authors.

[56]

Friday, September 20

This evening finds me bandaged and peevish – and
Vinnie's feline passion is the cause! She has now
brought three cats into the family – which is three
more than were invited. As I descended the last stair
on my way to the kitchen this morning, one of the

creatures flung itself beneath my feet and sent me
sprawling to the hall floor like a child from a sled. It
seemed a motiveless deed – but cats are inscrutable
beasts. Yesterday the miscreant protested when I
would not share the chicken parts needed for gravy.
It seems today she has taken her revenge. How I
miss poor Carlo's quiet company. He never willingly
caused grief to any.

I wrenched my ankle badly and had to spend the
day in bed. Vinnie bears remorse for two – since puss
is impenitent. Tonight the pain still throbs – too
much for thought.

Vinnie apparently always had cats for pets. In her last eccentric years,
when she was the only one living in the Homestead, she is reported to
have filled the house with as many as thirty. Emily was never particularly
fond of the animals. In a letter to Mrs. Holland in 1881 she noted that
Vinnie now had six cats "and finding Assassins for them, is my stealthy
Aim –." Emily's own beloved pet, her dog Carlo, had died in 1866.

[57]

Wednesday, September 25

*September has put on a glorious face for the Cattle
Show. The inspiriting air dissolved resistance – and
I accompanied the family to events today though I
am still slightly lame from Friday's mishap. In the
morning we watched the horses parade through the
Common as far as Main Street. Father was an
imposing figure on the black. In the afternoon he
made a speech, which many said was more enlight-
ening than those usually delivered. I doubt the event
could function without him!*

*The exhibitions were finer than ever. Many
excellent domestic items were entered. I particularly
enjoyed examining the quilts – bright bits of the past
stitched for the future. One was made by a six-year-
old child who had begun her task at the age of three!
The flame of creation has singed her early – I hope
it may continue to burn!*

*Mrs. Sweetser won a prize for her preserves.
As no Dickinson woman was represented this year,
we took our pride in neighboring accomplishments.
Mother had planned to display her fall flowers,*

which are lovely now, but her energy failed in the face of arrangement. Vinnie is content with the role of spectator. I no longer find satisfaction in awards for bread when yeastier creations consume my thought. But we all had an appetite for enjoyment – and judged it one of the best such events in many years.

On a par with Commencement as a highlight of the Amherst social calendar was the annual exhibition of the Hampshire Agricultural Society, commonly referred to as the "Cattle Show." In 1867 it was held on September 24 and 25. The *Express* reported that Edward Dickinson, designated "Father of the Society," was one of the speakers. The *Republican* noted his appearance on a "very showy black horse" in the morning cavalcade.

Mr. and Mrs. Luke Sweetser were lifelong neighbors of the Dickinsons.

In earlier years Emily sometimes entered her baked goods in the household competition. She won second prize for her rye and Indian bread in 1856.

Tuesday, October 1

A letter from Mr. Higginson arrived today. As if to
answer my unspoken question, he declares his desire
to "help me build my art and put my power to it's
fullest use." He says he values our warm friendship,
of which this aim is the foundation.

My teacher continues to urge a visit to Boston
where I could "meet the world" beyond Amherst
and find invigoration for my thoughts. He knows I
am occupied with "demands of home" and acknow-
ledges my "reluctance to travel" but hopes in time I
can be persuaded.

Mr. Higginson is a man of wide and eager
commerce with Society. He finds it hard to comprehend my little life – and has more than once wondered at it's lack of "activity." But is a Day to be
measured by motion? Must I be "of the world" to find
the poetry in it? So many horizons are bounded by
Happening – while Minds retreat. Thought is the
largest Event – How does one exist without? Sometimes the simplest life is the most complex. I live in
my Father's house but those walls do not confine me.

To meet my Friend would give me greatest pleasure
– but separation is too dear a price.

Higginson had just the previous year urged Emily to come to Boston for a literary gathering, but she refused the invitation, asking him to come to Amherst instead. He eventually visited her twice in Amherst, in 1870 and 1873.

[59]

Saturday, October 5

Vinnie left the household in my charge this after-
noon while she attended the wedding of her friend
Elizabeth. She wore her new gown – which adds
a quiet grace to her features. They are what persons
call handsome – but she only sees their faults – no
matter my assurances. The wedding she reports
was a gay affair and all found the bride and groom
well suited.

I often wonder whether Vinnie still hopes that
fate will similarly reward her. She never speaks of
her regrets – and the cruel game Love played at her

expense – but I know she has them. She might
reverse her life if she could but now she lives vigor-
ously in the present – accepting God's verdict. She is
too free-spirited to respect Opinion. In the town she
deals fearlessly with all. She seems content to command our household – which suits her I think
beyond all other calling. But if she chose another
house – she must take part of me with her – and I
do not care for travel! Thus – from selfish motive –
I do not let myself imagine the possibility.

In her late teens Vinnie fell in love with Joseph Lyman, a school friend of
Austin's, who she believed returned her affection. He left New England
in 1851, eventually taking up law practice in New Orleans. For several
years he continued to correspond with Vinnie and to entertain notions of
marrying her, but eventually he married someone else. Lyman was a frequent visitor to the Dickinson home during his college days, and his collected letters are a valuable source of information about the family and
particularly Emily, for whom he had great admiration. Although Vinnie
had a number of other suitors in her youth and apparently expected to
marry someday, she, like her sister, remained single all her life.

Monday, October 7

Father came home from the office this evening to
find a reading circle. Declaring that he was pleased
to see "minds at work," he inquired of each of us
what we read. Both Mother and Vinnie, sharing the
Republican, passed the test, but I had to confess to
Mrs. Browning, as the incriminating volume lay
on my lap. He frowned slightly and muttered,
"<u>Modern</u> poetry!"

   Poor Father. He is as solemn as his library.
Though he accepts Shakespeare and the poets of
earlier ages, he does not acknowledge the poetry
of Life itself. I know he does not thoroughly approve
of my efforts at verse, though he does not suspect
they are a passion. Because I am a woman, such
endeavors are not to be taken seriously but as I am
his daughter, whom I believe he loves in spite of our
unconnected courses, they must be allowed – if not
encouraged. For him the intellect of women ought to
be kept cooling in the cellar while manly thought
enjoys a heartier repast above stairs! His thoughts

about the proper role of woman he put in print some
years before my birth – and I guess he still feels the
same. For domestic pursuits – and no other – are we
suited, and though Education be broad and even
encouraged, it's aim is but the completer rendering of
household service.

Once he warned in direst terms of the conse-
quences for one who chooses a literary <u>wife</u>. It was
Father's misfortune to produce a literary <u>daughter</u> –
though thinking me the captive of whimsey, perhaps
he cannot guess the fullest horror of his deed!
Fortunately, he had already succeeded on his first
attempt – which lessens the sting of the second. In
Austin he has the son whose talents outshine the
stars! What by comparison are the pale jottings of
his daughter which he thinks not worthy of perusal?
Why then do I have so deep an affection for him –
that makes the thought of separation terrifying?

This entry provides a further example of the gulf that separated Emily
from her father—and of her desperate longing to bridge it. In 1826
and 1827 Edward Dickinson published a series of five essays on "Female

Education," under a pseudonym, in the *New England Inquirer,* an Amherst newspaper of the day. These had as their premise the idea that women operate in a different "sphere" from that of men. He warns that a man who wishes to be constantly instructed, criticized, and edified should be sure to choose a *"literary* wife." A modest and sweet disposition, he declares, along with "patience and forbearance and fortitude" will compensate for the lack of "brilliant talents."

 [61]

Thursday, October 10

Judge Lord is our welcome visitor tonight. Business of the courts takes him to Northampton and being so near Amherst he would not, as he said, "deny himself" a visit with the Dickinsons. Mrs. Lord is ill and did not accompany him.

He has for many years been a treasured friend to Father, with whom he shares a trait or two. But he yields more willingly to Life – who never surrendered to <u>us</u>. Laughter never hides when he is here. He enjoys a jest amidst his graver occupations. Though he toils – to exhaustion – in the world of men, his understanding goes beyond them. I feel it –

when we speak – and my heart is unsteady. I always
hope to hear more than he says. Am I still "little
Emily" or does his eye enlarge me now? I would –
when I write – share my best with him, but I fear to
replicate the past. Would he spurn the thought – or
mistake the sense? The cautious years – remembering
– whisper, "Futile!"

He told us at supper he would return in two
weeks and hoped to see us all again. I thought his
passing smile paused an instant on my face before it
surrounded the table.

It was not until the publication of Millicent Todd Bingham's *Emily Dickinson: A Revelation* (New York: Harper) in 1954 that concrete evidence was finally presented of at least one romantic relationship that Emily is known to have had. In this volume appeared fifteen letters and fragments (including both drafts and fair copies) that she wrote to Judge Otis Phillips Lord, a family friend eighteen years her senior (see No. 38), which clearly showed that she was in love with him and that the sentiment was returned. The letters (it is not known which of them were actually mailed), heavily censored by scissoring, had been given by Austin Dickinson to his lover, Mabel Loomis Todd, who later passed them on to her daughter. The first of these are assumed from the handwriting to have been written in 1878, after Mrs. Lord's death (in 1877), but it is apparent from this and later entries that Emily had begun to regard Judge Lord as more than a fatherly visitor long before that time. (See Nos. 65, 69, 77, 86, 90, and 100.)

During his distinguished career Lord served in the Massachusetts House of Representatives and Senate and on the state Superior Court before being appointed to the Supreme Judicial Court in 1875. He resigned in 1882 because of ill health, and died in 1884. The Lords had no children. After Mrs. Lord's death, her niece, Abbie Farley, kept house for the judge; she disapproved of his relationship with Emily Dickinson.

When the purpling afternoon
Shuts the offices of Care –
And you chamber up your thoughts –
Do I ever linger there?

Does your heart – a moment – halt
At the echo of my voice
When we spoke of all but Love
In so tremulous a peace?

Did my eyes betray a Hope
Visible to none but Thee?
Quickly – dearest! – whisper Yes –
That were Paradise to me!

[62]

Sunday, October 13

I had a letter from Mrs. Holland and dreamed of
her last night – then woke thinking of them both. As
this is the Sabbath I suppose they are at church if
the doctor resides in our geography. Their God is a
most congenial companion. They made an early
friend of Him and never fear to ask Him home for
tea. But He is circumspect and wont allow familiarity to all. He shows a thousand faces to those who
come before Him – boldly or on tiptoe. Father sees a
frown, Mother, eyes of compassion, Vinnie – lips
that bend to mirth. I steal a sly perspective and catch
a glimpse of all. The God revealed to Mr. Wadsworth is but a distant cousin of the Hollands'. Hide
and seek is our Creator's favorite game!

My thoughts I see have led me from the corn-
cakes. Now I hear Fathers stern summons – or
possibly the voice of God!

Dr. Holland, a well-known writer and lecturer (see No. 88), traveled
widely. After he died in October 1881, Emily wrote several letters of sympathy to his wife. In one of them she recalled her impressions during a

visit to their home many years before: "I shall never forget the Doctor's prayer, my first morning with you – so simple, so believing. *That* God must be a friend – *that* was a different God – and I almost felt warmer myself, in the midst of a tie so sunshiny."

 [63]

Friday, October 18

Fanny and Loo arrived this afternoon. Austin and Vinnie fetched them from the train. It is uncommon delight to have my little cousins close – if only for a few days. They are sweet and simple listeners. There was time today to explore the meadow – now denuded of crops – and feel the seasons changing. We talked until the dying light made us retreat. Both ends of day are frugal now. Gold vies everywhere with scarlet – and in the confusion – Summer has surrendered. Where she stood is only chill – and one departing Daisy. Death puts on it's colors and masquerades as Life. Each ruddy leaf partakes of both – as we ourselves in a gentler hour. Advent is only prelude to departure. The leaves – knowing – group for solace beneath my window to meet reviveless sleep.

For more on Fanny and Loo, see the note to No. 4.

Death is the door that swings two ways –
It double-hinges Life –
Unbidden – opens on our days –
As silent as a Grief –

Then arcs past Disbelief
Into it's alternate Domain,
Confiding where the ages go
Before it shuts – again.

To knock upon the Infinite –
Were futile as a plea
To turn the Revolution back
And halt Eternity –

The hour of Admission
Is hid beyond Surmise –
Where even Faith is impotent
To nominate the Close –

A sudden sweep – and we are drawn
Past latitudes of Fear –
Beyond retrieveless Boundaries
That marked our Heaven here.

 [64]

Wednesday, October 23

Vinnie has been invited by a woman in town to
join a ladies' society – to improve the world. Now her
head is full of suffrage and reforms – but I think she
may soon tire under their weight. Her passions are
changeable!

 Their efforts bring them honor – I should not
disapprove. But I do not harmonize with causes. Their
particularity constrains. Circumference – lets me sing
a wilder song than these.

The times are full of revolution. Making my own –
I need not join the common.

The notion that Emily Dickinson was an early "feminist," as the term is used today, is undercut by this entry, which reemphasizes a distance from social causes—including those particular to women—that is reflected in some of her letters and poetry and, indeed, in what is known about the general pattern of her life. In an early letter (1850) to her friend Jane Humphrey she characterized in sardonic terms the business of the local sewing society: "The Sewing Society has commenced again – and held its first meeting last week – now all the poor will be helped – the cold warmed – the warm cooled – the hungry fed – the thirsty attended to – the ragged clothed – and this suffering – tumbled down world will be helped to it's feet again – which will be quite pleasant to all. I dont attend – notwithstanding my high approbation – which must puzzle the public exceedingly. I am already set down as one of those brands almost consumed – and my hardheartedness gets me many prayers."

In 1872 Elizabeth Stuart Phelps, a well-known novelist and feminist and the editor of *The Woman's Journal*, wrote Emily to solicit her participation in some worthy cause—possibly through a piece of writing. Shortly thereafter Emily responded to a query about Phelps from her cousin Louise Norcross: "Of Miss P— I know but this, dear. She wrote me in October, requesting me to aid the world by my chirrup more. Perhaps she stated it as my duty, I don't distinctly remember, and always burn such letters, so I cannot obtain it now. I replied declining. She did not write to me again – she might have been offended, or perhaps is extricating humanity from some hopeless ditch. . . ." Emily Dickinson's interest, as this entry suggests, was in the larger issues of life, death, and faith, or as she told Higginson, "My Business is Circumference."

But if she had no inclination to join a political movement on behalf of women in general, it is clear that Emily keenly felt the effect that being a woman had on her own life and art. For these more personal views, see, for example, Nos. 16, 60, 70, and 95.

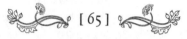

[65]

Sunday, October 27

What a holy Sabbath was this! Joy ran before it –
to prepare the way – when Judge Lord arrived as
promised last evening. We all gathered for tea in the
parlor – and had such an exchange of pleasantries
as Society could not disapprove.

But today brought a morning that might exceed
the bounds of Proper. For while the family were at
church – he came again. From my window I saw
him walking to our door. I heard his knock – and
was frightened – for there was no one to answer it.
I thought to hide but my heart had a kinder mes-
sage. I need not flee from him – indeed I cannot *–*
for thought of him arrests my will.

My hand trembled on the door and my soul felt
pallid when I admitted him. He said, "I knew the
others were gone to services but thought you said you
were a rare visitor there. A hope propelled my feet
from town – that you would be generous and consent
to see me a last time before I go. I must leave soon –
but wished to hear once more the sound of your
mind. Do you think me impertinent?"

How did he know his secret wish was mine? The
heart conceives a thought and paints it's image on
the face. I welcomed him then – for to do other were
not in contemplation. We lost the Present in a
depthless well where all Thought flowed together.

I have said it was Sunday. He has no church –
but worships in that grand cathedral whose dome is
morning and cornerstone the night. He sees the hand
of God in every day but cant profess to know the
why behind it's artful manipulations. He prays for
guidance and listens for directions. I guess he has a
keener ear than mine. We have met God in different
heavens – but today – in a parlor moment – the two
were one.

An hour was an instant. When he had gone I
thought he was a vision. He did not tell me – the

others might not understand our meeting – but the thought lay unspoken between us. It were needless to announce – I would not know how to share a bliss so deep.

The romance between Emily Dickinson and Judge Lord is assumed, on the basis of the fifteen letter drafts published in 1954 (see No. 61), to have begun openly after the death of his wife in 1877. However, most of the letters cannot be accurately dated, and some may have been written before that time. In any event, Emily's diary suggests that the foundation was being laid in 1867–68 for, if not a clandestine relationship, at least a secret correspondence that must have continued for ten years before culminating in an open romance. We have no evidence beyond these pages to indicate whether any other meetings such as the ones described here and in No. 100 ever occurred again, but it *is* known that Lord, after his appointment to the Superior Court in 1859, came to Northampton regularly in April and October. On some of these occasions he undoubtedly visited Amherst and may again have had a chance to converse with Emily alone.

There is a hint as to the ongoing nature of the relationship in the letter, tentatively dated 1878, that Johnson places first in his arrangement of the fifteen, in which Emily declares, "I have done with guises." Fragments of both a fair copy and a draft copy of the first letter in the series exist. The fair copy is reproduced following this entry.

In another of the letters Emily recounts a conversation she had with her nephew in which he asked whether Lord belonged to the church. She replied that Lord was not "technically" a member; "I think he does nothing ostensible." Elsewhere she told Lord, "While others go to Church, I go to mine, for are not you my Church, . . ."

STAMP

Pastiche Fine Desserts - Providence Rhode Island

(Letter 559, about 1878)

My lovely Salem smiles at me. I seek his Face so often – but I have done with guises.

I confess that I love him – I rejoice that I love him – I thank the maker of Heaven and Earth – that gave him me to love – the exultation floods me. I cannot find my channel – the Creek turns Sea – at thought of thee –

Will you punish me? "Involuntary Bankruptcy," how could that be Crime?

Incarcerate me in yourself – rosy penalty – threading with you this lovely maze, which is not Life or Death – though it has the intangibleness of one, and the flush of the other – waking for your sake on Day made magical with you before I went

(The rest of the letter is missing.)

[66]

Friday, November 1

Tonight I read a while from Mr. Emerson. I like to turn to him when the world feels clangorous – for then his harmonious vision relieves. He sees Nature forming a "perfect whole" with man. It is a joyous conceit – though disproved often by her less generous acts. Several years ago Austin and Sue entertained him in their parlor, surrounded by a host of earnest philosophers. I was invited to attend but did not –

feeling too small for the occasion. Often now I wish
our minds had spoken.

When I read "Each and All" I think of Newton
– for it was his favorite and my book was his. In my
greenest years of girlhood he showed me how to live
and told me I could be a poet. There was much I
never saw before he aimed my eyes. I miss him still
and the touch of his guiding hand. He left too soon
for proper parting. Yet his praise was sweet elixir –
and one sip gave me lasting strength.

Benjamin Franklin Newton became Emily's close friend while he was
studying law in her father's office between 1847 and 1849. (Emily was then
in her late teens.) He apparently steered her toward an appreciation of
literature and encouraged her poetry writing. Newton gave Emily a copy
of the 1847 edition of Emerson's *Poems*, marking the ones he thought best.
The quoted words in the first paragraph are from "Each and All."

Ben Newton married in 1851 after leaving Amherst. He and Emily probably continued to correspond, but none of their letters survive. He died
of consumption in 1853 at the age of thirty-two. In one of her early letters to Higginson, Emily said, "My dying Tutor told me that he would
like to live till I had been a poet, but Death was much of Mob as I could
master – then. . . ."

Thursday, November 7

Illness robbed me of the day – and diminished the
Future. How insidious are nature's Burglaries! The
body defies the spirit – which is willing but cannot
overcome the "too solid flesh."

For several days I have felt unwell, and yesterday
I could not rise from bed for the fever and chills.
They have subsided but left me too weak for creation.
Last week Mother suffered from the same though she
has mostly recovered. Father has a cough. Vinnie –
unfelled – tends to us all with good cheer.

Health is a visitor who has'nt called lately. How
welcome we should make her if she knocks again!

The allusions in the first paragraph are to Matthew 26:41 and *Hamlet*, act
I, scene 2.

Wednesday, November 13

Yesterday snow shrouded Amherst for the first time since the death of Summer. For several days the air was full of Implication – We knew it was not long until the first flake. A short thaw today was only enough to glaze the roads with ice. The children are already out coasting.

Beauty often dwells in desolation. The world goes in white to compensate for duller hues. The sun – emerging refreshed this morning – made the frozen branches sparkle like a jeweled city. Our "new earth" hints at Patmos' Jerusalem.

The reference is apparently to Revelation 21, where John of Patmos describes seeing "a new heaven and a new earth" and the "new Jerusalem, coming down from God out of Heaven." The new Jerusalem is pictured as a city made of gold and precious stones. Emily quoted frequently from Revelation, and chapter 21, which she called the "Gem chapter," was a favorite.

[69]

Friday, November 15

I read again before I sleep my letter from Judge Lord. He thanks me for our conversation on that happy Sunday, which meant he says "more than you surmise." How can I construe it? He finds "richest barter" in exchange of words because their value is intrinsic. Sometimes he puts the Law aside and takes a Shakespeare sonnet for his brief. Preparing an oration now occupies his chiefest hours. What pleasure do I have in words he asks beyond my speech and "captivating" letters.

Overwhelming question! I never answered it – before – fearing that he – like the others – might not wish to know so much. My feeling now – for him – is <u>unfamiliar</u> – because it may rebound upon the

*heart, beseeching more! But have I then another part
to give? I would not yield my Art – but if we two
might share – I could conjecture Paradise!*

Judge Lord enjoyed a reputation as an orator as well as a jurist. In one of
his speeches he described Shakespeare as the "great poet of nature,"
whose finest achievements were "his magnificent exhibitions of human
action." This love of Shakespeare and—as indicated in No. 69—of writing
and words in general was an obvious bond between Lord and Emily. Her
letters to him contain a number of allusions to Shakespeare's plays.

[70]

Thursday, November 21

*Reading tonight an essay from yesterday's Republi-
can – I felt again the old despair. It has the invinci-
bility of Malaria. The author of the stinging words –
whom I suppose to be Mr. Bowles – finds the
country "flooded" with "mistaken women-poets" –
"susceptible women" who think they were "born
artists" and "put themselves outside the pale of
domestic life and society which they naturally
require." Does he include me in their number? Has*

my life seemed to him no more than a frivolous
indulgence – denying that role for which my body –
but never my soul – was suited?

I need not flinch – now – for Truth made an
earlier wound. He has always mistaken Daisy, as
she once did him. She once hoped for a union of
minds – no other being possible – but time has
shown the folly of the dream. Affection finds it's own
level. So let us journey on through plains if we cant
reach the hills.

The article to which Emily refers, "Women as Artists," appeared in the November 20, 1867, issue of the *Republican* and was actually a tribute to the Cooper Institute for giving good instruction in painting to its female students. But she apparently construed its remarks about poets as giving the whole essay a wider application. Although it begins by saying, "Genius has no sex, according to its manifestations," the article later warns that the "only thing to be feared is that too many susceptible women will at once think they were born artists, and only need development, and will perhaps put themselves outside the pale of domestic life and the society which they naturally require, to nourish their mistaken endeavors. But the sensible women of taste will outnumber the foolish ones, and it will be no more terrible to have the country flooded with mistaken women-artists, so called, than with mistaken women-poets, who are so numerous lately."

Emily sometimes referred to herself as "Daisy," and in the third person, in her letters to Bowles. (Compare the language in the second and third Master letters, following No. 26.)

Love's jurisdiction never reached
Beyond one heart –
It's cause before the other tried
To heedless Court –

To ask for gold in change for pearl
Were futile aim –
Say then if <u>pearl</u> be worth the price –
Wherefore I come

Before a keener jury to direct
My Plea –
Submitting to the judgment
Of Eternity –

And should the Verdict favor – it
Were plainest Proof
That pearl and gold are synonym
In such a Life.

71

Tuesday, November 26

Tonight Austin arrived abruptly after another
meeting of the church committee to describe for us –
with his usual enthusiasm – how the new structure
is progressing. He insisted on leading me to the edge
of our grounds so that I might glimpse the building
through the now bare trees. The moon was unusually
bright and I could see the aspiring steeple outlined
against the sky. Standing so strong and full of hope
beneath that fathomless dark – it almost made me
wish to be among those it will eventually welcome.
At times I yearn for the surrounding strength of
Faith – but something prevents my surrender. I am
not suited for the panoply of full Confession. It's
weight is more than I can bear. I do not doubt God's
existence but fear his demands. If we yield to Him –
does it restrain – Ourselves? And yet have we the
power <u>not</u> to yield to One who knows our "downsit-
ting and uprising"?

The cornerstone for the new First Congregational Church in Amherst was laid in September 1867 on property that stood almost directly across the street from the Evergreens. Austin Dickinson played an important role in the promotion of the project and supervised the building's construction. A note in the *Express* for November 28 reported that the stonework was nearly complete. The church was dedicated in September 1868, with Edward Dickinson giving the dedicatory speech.

There is a legend, now confirmed by this entry, that Emily went with Austin one night as far as the hedge on her father's property to see the new church.

The quotation in the last line is from Psalm 139:2.

For more on Emily's early refusal to undergo a religious conversion, see the note to No. 3.

Heaven! Would you welcome one
Who never dared to sell
All that she had to follow Him?
That Barter of the Soul

As foreign to capacity
As singing to the dead –
A Trade retrieveless as a tune
From lips forever stilled –

But if a step be hazarded –
Surrender incomplete –
Then might a humbler door admit
Those bold returning Feet?

72

Thursday, November 28

Thanksgiving Day. Vinnie and I were up long before dawn to complete the preparations begun yesterday for our traditional feast. Mother came down later to supervise. Father and Austin set work aside and both houses gathered for an afternoon of unaccustomed merriment. We spread so many dishes the table could scarcely hold them – stuffed turkey, rice, squash, and vegetables preserved from the summer garden, two fresh loaves of rye and Indian bread, and clear beef soup – both "gifts" of Mrs. Child – and plenty of currant wine. I made three mince pies, which everyone declared "unexcelled." This is the only day of the year on which Father will countenance such excesses! If Gluttony is a measure of our thanks to God, then He was well satisfied! But food and love are intimate companions. Gathered here – on such a day – we feel the proof of that.

In mid-nineteenth-century New England, Thanksgiving was a more important holiday than Christmas. One of the staples in the Dickinson household was the cookbook *The Frugal Housewife*, by Lydia Maria Child, given by Edward Dickinson to his wife in 1832.

 [73]

Monday, December 2

Father left this morning for Northampton and a few days business. Our evenings are strange without him. We are more casual at supper – abandoning his rigid schedule – but we feel a bit uneasy at the flexibility!

The childhood memories remain. In those days when he was gone, it seemed the household was in gentle disarray – the merest chair awaited his return for imposition of the former order. It was a curious sensation – for his absence gave our spirits greater freedom – There was less wrath to risk! Yet I always looked forward to his return – and to his letters if the separation was long. He used to write to just us children and made his words as tender as he had the power to do. I liked to think the act was more than duty and that missing our faces – though he never said – he called them forth upon the page. No colorful displays marked his return, but I felt the joy – he could not express – when he saw his children run to welcome.

Perhaps I feel his absence so because we two are similar. Seeing ourselves – in each other – we fear to bring the common mirror closer. We both wear a vail – though our purposes are different. I hide from the world but Father – who confronts the world – hides from his own soul – and from the family that would define him.

He holds affection in abeyance – as though awaiting a suitable moment for bestowment. We follow him in this – for the pattern was set – but though lips be silent, hearts speak quietly.

An example of the kind of letter that Emily remembers so fondly in this entry follows: "My Dear Little Children, I am glad to hear that you have been so good little children, since I left home – I want to have you see which of you will be the best – . . . Be kind & pleasant to Mother, & each other – do exactly as she tells you – . . . Now you must learn, & study, to do as Mother wants you to – She will always do exactly right by you. Good night.

Your dear father, E. Dickinson" (quoted by Jay Leyda in *The Years and Hours of Emily Dickinson*, vol. 1, p. 41, published by Yale University Press in 1960).

Late in her life Vinnie described the members of her family as having lived "like friendly and absolute monarchs, each in his own domain" (from Millicent Todd Bingham, *Emily Dickinson's Home*).

 [74]

Thursday, December 5

This evening I discovered Mother at her writing
table with pen in hand and a little book before her.
The pen – suspended in air – seemed detached from
her, uncertain of it's course. Curiosity overcame me
and I asked her what she wrote. She told me she had
decided to begin a diary "for posterity." Austin's
children might someday want to know – how we
lived – and she would let them see it through her eyes.

Wonder overtook me – to find our natures joined
by this common spark. For all our years it has been
hidden – a quiet flicker in some dusty corner of the
household. Now I know of it's existence – but Mother
never will. I have told no one about <u>my</u> diary. I
shrink from display of such a portrait for those I love

– lest I disturb the colors they themselves have chosen.
These pages must be preserved – like ripe fruit in a
jar – and sealed until a more susceptible day.

I am amused – but tenderly – by Mother's hopeful
occupation. Words never had a magic for her. To
write a letter is a daunting task. Yet I believe she
<u>wants</u> to savor thought – if she might be directed to
it's avenues. Perhaps she thinks this daily chronicle
will be her guide.

I praised her for an excellent idea and offered my
encouragement. I wish I had a better gift. Mother has
given to the family all that she could spare. Often we
forgot the child that needed nurture in return.

Much has been written about the relationship between Emily and her
mother, Emily Norcross Dickinson. As in the case of her father, one re-
ceives conflicting impressions from Emily's own contradictory descriptions. In her second letter to Higginson she wrote, "My Mother does
not care for thought." By Higginson's account of their 1870 meeting, she
stated, "I never had a mother. I suppose a mother is one to whom you
hurry when you are troubled." Yet many of her letters, particularly those
written to Austin in the 1850s, show a pleasant woman concerned about
her family and busy with household tasks for their benefit.

See also Nos. 84 and 94.

Tuesday, December 10

I have completed my thirty-seventh year. Austin and
Sue came for tea to mark the occasion, leaving the
children with the Newmans. They brought another
offering from Mr. Dickens for my library. Vinnie
and Mother made chicken salad and gold and silver
cake. Family concord is the greatest gift!

Will any mark this day when Dickinsons no
longer gather? Life and I have had a sturdier
friendship than that granted to many. Great
numbers of the ones I loved she has abandoned.
Who elected me for farther knowledge? I never
stop wondering – why I am myself – and not a
robin! That we live at all is amazing. Events are
only details to color the Mystery, all tomorrows
but Surmises.

More often now I hear the pounding of the days
as they race toward Conclusion. I cant let them pass
without taking something for the Future.

The Dickens volume may have been *Little Dorrit,* the eighth volume of a set known as "Diamond Dickens," which became available in October.

[76]

Friday, December 13

Gloom overtook the day – and a chill lingered through the fires. When Nature lowers, the soul stands rigid. A gray horizon makes the most harmless chore a burden and tedium reigns. Mother spent the day in bed, beset by a cold and fever. Father was more querulous than usual. Vinnie outpaced the weather. Busy at embroidery, she stitched happily all afternoon, oblivious of the clouds.

After supper I fled to poetry, which redeems the dreariest hour. Once a verse is complete, I feel relieved of a burden. During the night the lines often wake me – The feet throb in my brain and the words claim my breath. Then I know what the World does not – another name for Love.

The Bliss that ends Despair
Is deeper than the one
That hearts accustomed title Glee
And value with the Sun

A consummation nobler
Than Nature ever showed
Her ardent creatures – is the Soul's
Possession by the Word.

No bee drawn by a nectar
Or robin to the nest
Conceives a passion like the Song
Spilled from a Poet's breast.

Wednesday, December 18

A letter to Judge and Mrs. Lord consumed my
evening. I speak to both – but my thoughts are
chiefly for him – who may more willingly hear. The
season requires remembrance – and it makes me
bold. In the guise of gift I enclose three poems. I
never dared before. Will he find the presumption too
large? How strange to fear the sending that is so
natural with others. But they are light recipients.
Now expectation bears heavier possibilities. Approval
– beyond courtesy – is a timid hope. Silence hurts
most. But I have often sung before the deaf.

See also Nos. 69 and 86.

Friday, December 20

A glance at the Republican completes my day.
Several poems are there – but none made me tremble.
Last year my "narrow fellow" escaped to those pages
– unknown to his creator – and twisted from his
shape. My verse must shine in it's own light –
without another's burnishing. If not – I keep them in
the shadows until a brighter day. Reading – for the
blind – is idle occupation. Greatness is patient.

Only six of Emily's poems appeared in the *Republican* during her lifetime, all anonymously and most with added titles and alterations. The one referred to here, "A narrow Fellow in the Grass" (986), was written in 1865 and a copy probably given to Sue. Johnson speculates that it was Sue who forwarded her copy to Samuel Bowles, who published it in February 1866. Emily protested to Higginson that the poem had been "robbed" from her and the punctuation changed, adding, "I had told you I did not print – I feared you might think me ostensible."

Reemphasizing her wary attitude toward publication, she seems in this entry to offer a rationale for it and to suggest an eventual solution.

In 1870 she wrote to Higginson, "Thank you for Greatness – I will have deserved it in a longer time!"

See also Nos. 19 and 101.

(986)

A narrow Fellow in the Grass
Occasionally rides –
You may have met Him – did you not
His notice sudden is –

The Grass divides as with a Comb –
A spotted shaft is seen –
And then it closes at your feet
And opens further on –

He likes a Boggy Acre
A Floor too cool for Corn –
Yet when a Boy, and Barefoot –
I more than once at Noon
Have passed, I thought, a Whip lash
Unbraiding in the Sun
When stooping to secure it
It wrinkled, and was gone –

Several of Nature's People
I know, and they know me –
I feel for them a transport
Of cordiality –

But never met this Fellow
Attended, or alone
Without a tighter breathing
And Zero at the Bone –

[79]

Wednesday, December 25

Christmas Day – as holy in feeling as Sunday – but more joyous! We observed it more quietly than usual as Austin and Sue – with the children – are in New York visiting Sue's relatives. Vinnie accepted the invitation to join them. I believe they will also see Peter. Vinnie returns tomorrow. Father spared himself a half day of labor so that we might enjoy an afternoon together and exchange our few gifts. The Newmans – having no one in their charge – were free to celebrate with us. Father thinks highly of them – and I notice how he brightens in their presence. I sent them home with a fruitcake – just for themselves.

There is more of a festive air about town than formerly. There was to be a Christmas festival last night in North Amherst. Sue's laurel wreaths now incite fewer remarks! I enjoy the trappings of the holiday. Why should so momentous a birth not be gaily celebrated? Solemnity and sorrow await us at the other side of the year.

Christmas at this time was only beginning to be celebrated as a holiday more on a par with Thanksgiving or Easter instead of simply a day of solemn religious observance. According to Martha Dickinson Bianchi, after her parents' marriage, Sue put laurel wreaths in their windows at Christmas, which caused their Puritan neighbors to accuse Austin of having married a Catholic.

Perez Cowan recorded in his diary for December 25 that he had had Christmas dinner with Sue and Austin in "N.Y." (the entry suggests that this might have been Geneva, New York, where Sue had grown up under the care of an aunt after the death of her parents), that "Coz Lavinia" was there, and that he had seen her off on the train the next day.

 [80]

Friday, December 27

The sky was heavy – and the winds howled all day.
This afternoon another of the town's children was
laid to rest. The Johnsons' baby, Jessie, only ten
months old, died after a sudden illness. Mother went
to the funeral. She always visits the dead with grace.
Others depend on her compassion, which is never
ostensible. Mother said that the child's pure coffined
face wore a "hopeful expression" – as if anticipating a
second chance at life.

So many are robbed of an earth they have scarcely
trod upon. What cruel plan calls for youth's destruc-
tion? God's hand strikes without discrimination. Is
He then merciful, as the Pulpits proclaim? In a Life
where knowing is denied, nothing remains but hope
of Immortality – on earth as in heaven. To cheat
Death is my occupation.

The death of the Johnson child on December 21 was recorded in the January 2 issue of the *Express.*
   See Nos. 74 and 84 for notes on Mrs. Dickinson.

Refusal was a blank endeavor –
As futile as the ageless Fight –
But still we struggled – until Morning
Redeemed the unforgiving night –

He stronger was than I – but yielding
To his intractable embrace –
I was the shrewder – hiding Treasure –
Beyond his sight – to mark my place.

 [81]

The calendar issues it's annual challenge. Father
turned sixty-five today. I prepared Homestead
Charlotte Russe, one of his favorites, but he
wanted no other celebration than a quiet evening
with the family. He put his briefs aside in favor
of a gentler occupation. Austin and Sue were called
to an "obligatory" social occasion and could not join
us four.

We talked of trifling matters – for Life is not
<u>always</u> weighty – and laughed at Vinnies mimicry
of local personages. I read one or two amazing tales
from the Republican. Do so many live such extraordinary lives? Father allowed himself to be amused.
He does not always acknowledge levity – but
sometimes it strikes him unawares!

To welcome the New Year with jollity – Life's
simplest anodyne – is propitious beginning. Ourselves – like the years – are renewable.

Monday, January 6

I have been rereading my preceptor's article in the
Atlantic. It both teaches and troubles. He urges effort
by the poet – to achieve simplicity through pruning.
The first crop – he says – must be ploughed. It's
plain he thinks an eccentric gardener cant produce a
perfect fruit! Does he mean <u>me</u> – to find a mirror in
his words? Again I wonder what I am to him.

I cannot hold to strict obedience of his rules.
Many lines I shape and govern – but others are
despatched like Melody on the wind – and who can
tame that Tune? It is inner than craft. This is the
magic he cant understand and never will I fear.

But to test his thought against my own invigo-
rates. His mind and character fascinate and separate
him from the many. To know he will respond –
when I bring my life to him – is ample recompense
for the exertion. He is a Friend – For that I hope
and persevere. Familiarity may breed fondness!

Another of Higginson's frequent articles appeared in the December 1867 issue of the *Atlantic*. In "Literature as an Art," he argued that simplicity "must be the first element of literary art" and declared that "eccentricity, though often promising as a mere trait of youth, is only a disfigurement to maturer years. . . . A young writer must commonly plough in his first crop. . . ."

The melody/wind imagery in the second paragraph recalls poem 321, "Of all the Sounds despatched abroad" (1862), often interpreted as a metaphor for poetic inspiration.

(321)

Of all the Sounds despatched abroad,
There's not a Charge to me
Like that old measure in the Boughs –
That phraseless Melody –
The Wind does – working like a Hand,
Whose fingers Comb the Sky –
Then quiver down – with tufts of Tune –
Permitted Gods, and me –

Inheritance, it is, to us –
Beyond the Art to Earn –
Beyond the trait to take away
By Robber, since the Gain
Is gotten not of fingers –
And inner than the Bone –
Hid golden, for the whole of Days,
And even in the Urn,
I cannot vouch the merry Dust

Do not arise and play
In some odd fashion of its own,
Some quainter Holiday,
When Winds go round and round in Bands –
And thrum upon the door,
And Birds take places, overhead,
To bear them Orchestra.

I crave Him grace of Summer Boughs,
If such an Outcast be –
Who never heard that fleshless Chant –
Rise – solemn – on the Tree,
As if some Caravan of Sound
Off Deserts, in the Sky,
Had parted Rank,
Then knit, and swept –
In Seamless Company –

[83]

Thursday, January 9

Father read that Judge Lord recently addressed a
convocation of his fellows. He raised the subject at
table tonight – and I felt a strange chill at the
mention. He was full of compliments for his friend –
whose life I sometimes think he would take for his

own. He envies the judge his travels and distinctions
– but bears him no ill will for that and always
praises him highly. Father frequently surpasses
understanding. All who know him hold no one above
in accomplishment – but he himself will not acknowledge it.

He and his old friend share more than paths.
Perhaps it is the love for one that draws me toward
the other. How amusing to observe – The Law has
followed me all my days as if to ferret my secret
chambers – and impose on me the heavy hand of
Regulation! Had I been born a man – and forced to
a profession – perhaps it would have mastered me
completely. Molded to the family pattern – how could
I escape!

See Nos. 40, 47, and 85 for notes on the Dickinson legal careers.

Sunday, January 12

Sunday afternoon. Our fires blaze against a quartz
landscape. So piercing is the air I was glad to feel no
obligation to accompany the others to church this
morning. Mother did'nt go, feeling less capable and I
guess less spiritual than usual. She rested in her
room, emerging now and then to observe lest my toils
sully the Sabbath. My frequent Sunday scribbling
she might see as sacrilege – but even Mother must
make allowances for the preparation of dinner! Does
not God himself? We must have loaves and fishes
with our sermons.

Sue and Austin stopped in after the service but
did'nt stay to dinner despite Father's urging that
they fetch the children and return. They thought it
not convenient to do so today with the temperature so
arctic and Mattie with a cold. Father looks for every
opportunity to spend more time in conversation with
Sue. I think the brief visit cheered Mother. Austin
always finds a way to amuse her.

Society is a tonic for her. She prefers the company
of others to the delights of the mind. On a day when

winter is at it's most unyielding and prevents
visiting, she wears a vail of discontent. Her strength
– never large – then fails her the more.

Mother always excelled in domestic arts. Some-
times I worry that she feels Vinnie and I have
usurped her role in the household – though she
would not suggest it. But she tires too easily now to
manage affairs by herself. Does she therefore think
we value her less? I would reassure her – if I knew
how to do it. Exchange of thought between us was
never easy. Mother and daughter share the love that
nature planned – but we inhabit different realms.

Although, as we saw in No. 74, Mrs. Dickinson had no particular interest in intellectual pursuits, she was, at least in the early days, an excellent cook and housekeeper and took an active part in the community, serving on committees for the Cattle Show, doing work for the church, and serving as hostess for the annual Commencement teas. She seems to have been a sociable person, as this entry indicates and as is apparent in some of Emily's other comments ("Mother misses power to ramble to her Neighbors – and the stale inflation of the minor News"). On one occasion she went to a party "for married people"—without her husband.

From the 1850s on, Mrs. Dickinson suffered episodes of ill health from unspecified causes, though it was not until she had a stroke in 1875 that she actually became an invalid, requiring constant care from Emily and

Vinnie. These years of caretaking drew Emily closer to her mother, and her letters after Mrs. Dickinson's death in 1882 give evidence of a deep tenderness. To Mrs. Holland she wrote, "We were never intimate Mother and Children while she was our Mother – but Mines in the same Ground meet by tunneling and when she became our Child, the Affection came – ." This diary entry suggests that the affection, if not so dramatically expressed until late in Emily's own life, was always latent in the relationship.

[85]

Thursday, January 16

Austin has just left. More and more often he pays these evening visits, which he seems to find as soothing as the tea we give him. How fortunate <u>we</u> are that he never ceased to love his first home – but I regret for his sake that it now surpasses the second in his affection. He says nothing directly but we know he is not happy with his domestic arrangement. He wearies of Sue's pace. Social intercourse is for him more duty than pleasure. He would rather listen to the sounds of a summer day than the hum of a drawing room.

We are solace for him. He and I were perhaps never closer than now, though we still stand a small distance from a true meeting of minds. I cant confess to him that Poetry is my life – and he does not admit that he would rather have been a Poet! He could not escape his heritage. Like Father and Grandfather he was born with a sense of duty fully developed, which now weighs heavily on him. He feels himself indispensable to the community but half wishes it were not so. Once he confided to me that the Law no longer speaks to him as clearly as when he first answered it's call.

When our path wanders into a dark wood, how hard it is to retrace the steps that led us there. Return is foreclosed where the Road is preordained. Life is our Contract – and none but the highest Court may set it aside.

William Austin Dickinson eventually became as much of a leading light in the Amherst community as his father and grandfather before him. Samuel Fowler Dickinson, also a prominent lawyer, was a principal force behind the founding of Amherst Academy and Amherst College, and the unstinting monetary support he gave to the effort eventually drove him to financial ruin. The Dickinson-Amherst connection was continued in his son Edward's long service as treasurer of the college and then by Austin's in the same position. During Austin's tenure as treasurer, he oversaw the landscaping of the college grounds and the addition of several new buildings. A lover of nature, he devoted much of his time to the beautification of the town common. He was also on the boards of several companies and supervised the construction of the First Congregational Church in 1867–68 (see No. 71).

Although Austin followed in his father's footsteps by joining him in the practice of law, he was quite a different person from Edward. He was a more sociable figure, known for his flamboyant dress and behavior. He read widely and had a passion for collecting art. There is even the suggestion, in one of Emily's early letters to him, that he had tried his hand at writing poetry.

As pointed out in the notes to Nos. 9 and 20, Austin's home life was not happy. His marriage to Sue proved disastrous, and although he was close to his young son Gilbert, whose death in 1883 was a severe blow to him, he was always estranged from his other two children. In 1881 Austin became acquainted with Mabel Loomis Todd, wife of David Peck Todd, who had been appointed director of the Amherst College Observatory. The couple had moved to Amherst from Washington, D.C. Mrs. Todd was a writer, musician, and artist and was soon much in demand for social and cultural events in the town. By the end of 1882 she and Austin had begun a passionate love affair that lasted until Austin's death in 1895. It was largely through Mabel Todd's efforts that Emily Dickinson's poems finally became known to the world.

He drew the terms
Our Life defined –
And bargainless –
At birth we signed –
Forever bound
By that grave pact
We sealed in one
Unwitting act –
Of which no Revocation be –
Except –
Through Immortality.

 [86]

Tuesday, January 21

I have thought all this day that I was dreaming.
Duties dissolved and the January sky – gray to the
world – was gold to me. In the morning the post
brought a letter from Judge Lord and – unsealing –
began my bliss. The words speak little of events but
much of emotion. Thanking me for the verses I sent
at Christmas, he begs forgiveness for delaying his
reply. Most of his hours are stolen by the courts.

He says, "From the days of our first acquaintance I saw how fine is the habitation in which you dwell, and your Christmas messages are the proof. Your small world belies your vision. Few could picture death as well as you, not having been to the place, or capture life's simplest beauties in the summer storm. Indeed, your sight is 'double-hinged'!"

Dare I hope we <u>share</u> a vision? If his understanding be real, ours were a harmony undreamed of. His acceptance is my Crown.

The references in Lord's letter make it clear that the poems Emily sent him were from this diary.

[87]

Tuesday, January 28

I passed Father's library tonight and – through the open door – saw him frowning – in great concentration – at the volume on his lap. I suspected at first some legal tome but then saw it was the family Bible. Father says he gains much strength from scripture.

I guess he finds a companion in it's Author. He sees
God as his partner in the practice of life. I sense he
is uneasy with the thought – that God should master
him completely!

I remember – when barely gone from infancy and
the pastor on Sunday prayed to "Our Father who art
in Heaven" – I thought he spoke of my own father –
the only one I knew – and wondered where his
heaven was. I never asked the question – for children
make a habit of perplexity – till time erases it. That
was a child's confusion – but the woman now
perceives the similarity! Two fathers – earthly and
divine – whose austere countenance oversees our
days. Neither suffers proximity – and return of love
is only known by faith.

It is reported that when Edward Dickinson underwent a religious conversion in 1850, his pastor admonished, "You want to come to Christ as a *lawyer*—but you must come to him as a *poor sinner*—get down on your knees
& let me pray for you, & then pray for yourself" (quoted in Jay Leyda's
Years and Hours of Emily Dickinson 1:178).

Monday, February 3

Mrs. Holland writes that she and the doctor will
come the week after next when he is to speak at the
Village Church. They will certainly pass some time
with us. I almost tremble at the thought. As dear as
they are to me – particularly little Mrs. Holland – I
have grown less comfortable with visitors – even those
I love – and shun encounters lest we disappoint each
other's expectations. The real startles the ideal.

The voice of a letter is inciting music – but
corporeity intimidates. Love is shaped – with words –
more easily than face to face. I would not offer less
than gold – but fear depleted mines.

Dr. Josiah Holland was much in demand as a speaker, and the February 13
issue of the *Hampshire Express* announced that he would be in Amherst
February 18 to deliver a lecture on the "Woman Question" for the benefit
of the Ladies Society of Grace Church Parish. (See No. 95.)

Though trained as a physician, Holland gave up the practice of medi-
cine after only two years and eventually gained a national reputation as a
writer, critic, and editor. At the time this entry was written, he was part
owner of the *Springfield Republican,* where he became famous, under the
pen name Timothy Titcomb, as the author of a series of advice articles

about moral issues directed to unmarried men and women and young married couples.

In 1870 Holland founded *Scribner's Monthly*. As its editor, he encouraged new writers, but no poems of Emily Dickinson ever appeared there. Holland was quoted by a friend of Emily's as having said that her poetry was "too ethereal" for publication. There is no record that Emily ever turned to him for literary advice (except for the hint in No. 34) and no indication, in the letters or elsewhere, that either he or his wife recognized her genius.

 [89]

Sunday, February 9

Winter will not relinquish it's crown. Snow hides the earth and – in the bitter air – the trees stand stiff. A pale sun appeared this afternoon but soon ceded it's position. Yet inside jessamine and crocus – fearless – smile, while purple blossoms make a bold display. Life blooms undeterred though it glimpse Death through the window. I find peace in this indoor garden. My flowers – Nature's emissaries – nod approvingly as my pen moves – and knowing that – it moves more quickly!

As explained in the prologue, Emily's diary was discovered in the conservatory on the east side of the Homestead, one of her favorite spots. Her niece, Martha Bianchi, described it as a "fairyland" at all seasons, a tiny glass room with white shelves on one wall, on which grew ferns, heliotrope, jasmine, and other varieties of exotic plants.

The *Express* for February 13, 1868, reported temperatures of fourteen to twenty degrees below zero that week.

 [90]

Sunday, February 16

It is very late. I have written Judge Lord to thank
him for the kindness in his recent letter. My heart I
opened but halfway. He is not free to enter nor I to
leave thereafter. Awe makes me silent. I have let him
see me as a Poet – but never can as Woman. His
words speak admiration. I dare not presume beyond
– though Intuition pulls me toward a feathered hope.
So I leave off waking thoughts and let him pass the
portals of my dreams.

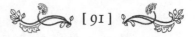

Saturday, February 22

I spent this evening writing letters to friends I have
not spoken to for many weeks. Events are haphazard
– the words must shape them. As the conversation
progresses, my thoughts – impatient – speed on – too
quick for my pen. Then I fear they will scatter to the
corners and escape to Eternity! I read that Branwell
Bronte could write two letters at once on two
different subjects! Enviable talent! But does each
friend thereby receive only half as much attention?

The anecdote about Branwell Brontë was reported in an article on the
front page of the *Express* for February 20.

Tuesday, February 25

On his visit this evening Austin reported much
progress on the church. It was late when he arrived
and the others were ready to retire. After they said
their goodnights, he and I talked softly in the dining
room. He confessed it is only now that he feels at one
with the congregation – after so many years as a
member of it. I never suspected what he told me –
that he always felt his conversion a false and
constrained act and a betrayal of himself. He envied
me my refusal to submit while <u>I</u> regretted I could <u>not</u>
and thought myself damned! But now after his long
labors on behalf of the new building, his soul is
serene. It is not a happiness I completely understand,
for I am still a Wanderer, but I rejoice in any ray
that brightens his dim life.

For more on the building of the church, see No. 71, and for a biographical
sketch of Austin, see the note to No. 85. Emily's attitude toward formal
religion is explored more fully in No. 3 and the accompanying note.

Sunday, March 1

Last night I dreamed I climbed a hill toward God.
Along a tortuous path cruel branches snatched at my
face – and stones cut my feet. Crying out – I turned
back – recanting my journey – but where the road
had been I saw only a yawning pit. Two choices met
me – to plunge into the Darkness or struggle toward
Heaven. Imitating Sisyphus, I turned once more
upward – clutching at the rocks for balance. When I
stumbled and slipped to earth, a demon chorus raised
a horrifying laugh. Then – almost at the pinnacle –
I heard God's voice – but fainter than He sounded
in the Bible. From the center of a distant light He
spoke my name. My feet forgot their heaviness and I
rushed forward. I started to reply – but awoke – to
a dark as deep as that preceding Genesis. The silence
was heavier than sleep – and I could not distinguish
the dream. A longing overcame me – and I prayed –
in unaccustomed tones – to hear the voice again.

No date has been assigned to Emily's poem 1712, "A Pit – but Heaven over it – ," but it may have been written about the time she had the dream described here.

In Greek mythology Sisyphus was the king of Corinth, punished in the Underworld for his earthly sins by constantly having to push a stone up a hill, only to have it roll back down again before it reached the top.

(1712)
A Pit – but Heaven over it –
And Heaven beside, and Heaven abroad,
And yet a Pit –
With Heaven over it.

To stir would be to slip –
To look would be to drop –
To dream – to sap the Prop
That holds my chances up.
Ah! Pit! With Heaven over it!

The depth is all my thought –
I dare not ask my feet –
'Twould start us where we sit
So straight you'd scarce suspect
It was a Pit – with fathoms under it –
Its Circuit just the same.
Seed – summer – tomb –
Whose Doom to whom?

94

Monday, March 9

This evening Mother and Father went to a party to celebrate the twentieth anniversary of Mr. and Mrs. Cowles. Mother looked like a fresh flower in her new dress. The prospect of company puts health in her cheek. Father appeared distinguished as usual – and quite prepared for a speech should the occasion demand! They have not yet returned though the hour is late. For Father the glitter quickly wears off a social gathering. It is a compliment to the Cowleses that they have remained so long. I hope both he and Mother found amusement tonight. I like to imagine them sharing joy openly – Their individual pleasures are so different. Mother participates happily in events but has'nt Father's ability to command them.

I often wonder what they talk about when the family are not there to guide the conversation. What force drew them together? I guess she needed Father's strength to mold her while he, being shaped already, sought a gentle reflector for his light. His presence is forbidding – though it conceal a softer nature – but Mother's genuine sweetness lights her surface. They

*are a strange couple, but the love between them is
beyond Display.*

*Vinnie spent the evening reading Harpers until she
began to doze in the chair and recognized futility. The
house was so still my thoughts had a larger sound
than customary. I opened my mind and let them escape
to the Page.*

Edward Dickinson's letters to Emily Norcross during their courtship
suggest an absence of passion but a commonsense appreciation of the
admirable qualities she possessed that would make her a good wife, such
as an "amiable disposition," a modest manner, and a thorough knowledge
of "domestic economy." Edward was in favor of education for women and
once observed that it was the wife more than the husband who gave character to the house and family, but in view of his ideas about a woman's
proper role and his aversion to the prospect of a "literary wife" (see
No. 60), it is a fair assumption that he felt completely safe in his choice of
Emily Norcross. Whether she was intimidated by his imperious style
throughout their marriage or merely bore it with traditional nineteenth-
century wifely equanimity can never be known, but her daughter's comments here suggest the latter conclusion. In a letter to Mrs. Holland in
1881, Emily reported that her mother had said after Edward's death, "I
loved him so."

 [95]

Thursday, March 12

Last Friday evening Dr. Holland finally made his appearance at the church – long postponed because of his brother's sudden death. Mrs. Holland did not come, and his visit was so brief we did not see him. The subject of the speech was the "Woman Question." I did not attend but the Express gives a full account. The church was filled to hear the address – which seems to have met with general favor. There is much discussion these days of whether women ought to be allowed to vote. The question does not entice me. Affairs of state ride beyond my door – I only note their progress. But why should sex determine who may join the march?

Dr. Holland opposes the extension of suffrage, but it is his larger implication that disquiets me. For him woman has but one legitimate role – that of homemaker, preserver of the family. He asserts, "All men and all women were intended for marriage." "Family is a divine institution" upon which everything else of value in the world depends. Does he then think the less of those whom marriage never

called? If I have not helped to "purify the state"
through propagation, are my peculiar fruits too poor
for counting? I believe there are but few men who
know how to put "soul before sex" as Mr. Higginson
once admonished. Newton was one – for he loved
what I could be as much as what I am – and Austin
– in his freer moments – can value sexless intellect.
Now I rejoice in my new friend – who sets no
boundaries for Possibility. The others only pretend,
thinking us "too light a book for a grave man's
reading." Opinion stings – but never did deter me.
My Stream charts it's own course. To be a Woman is
ordained – I need not pause for the condition. I have
no rank but Poet – a Title to surpass all others.

The *Express* reported on February 20 that Dr. Holland's speaking engage-
ment, scheduled for February 18, had been postponed, as Emily notes,
because of his brother's death. The lecture was finally given on March 6.

The Higginson quotation is from an article he wrote for the February
1859 issue of the *Atlantic Monthly,* "Ought Women to Learn the Alpha-
bet?" a plea on behalf of women's rights ("Soul before sex. Give an equal
chance, and let genius and industry do the rest . . .").

The last quotation is from *Aurora Leigh,* V, 41 (see No. 16).

The last line of the entry may allude to poem 1072, "Title divine – is mine!" (written about 1862).

(1072)

Title divine – is mine!
The Wife – without the Sign!
Acute Degree – conferred on me –
Empress of Calvary!
Royal – all but the Crown!
Betrothed – without the swoon
God sends us Women –
When you – hold – Garnet to Garnet –
Gold – to Gold –
Born – Bridalled – Shrouded –
In a Day –
Tri Victory
"My Husband" – women say –
Stroking the Melody –
Is *this* – the way?

Sunday, March 15

This was a remarkable day. In the afternoon I sat in
the conservatory surrounded by colors and borgeon-
ing blooms rereading a letter from Fanny and Loo.
Dinner was finished and a Sunday peace settled over
all, assuaging the bitter chill of outdoors. Vinnie and
Mother dozed in the parlor and Father I thought
was reading in his study. A verse cried for release
and I began to scribble on the back of the envelope.
Suddenly Father entered and inquired what I was
doing. "Writing a few lines, Father," I replied. "A
letter then?" "No, just a bit of verse." "So you fancy
yourself a poet, do you?" "I enjoy the pursuit of
words, Father – when household business dont
summon me first." He hesitated as if trying to decide
whether to continue. "Sue has spoken to me of your
verses. I am no judge of poetry – but do you think I
might see one?"

Father amazes me often but never more than this
afternoon. Until today he had never expressed an
interest in how I spend my "idle" moments and I
supposed he thought the occupation – if he knew of

it – a squandering of hours. He himself no longer
pauses for a sunset. I showed him these eight lines.
When he finished reading, his face revealed nothing
– but I thought I saw a small unbidden gleam of
pleasure in his eyes. He said only, "You have used
what you were given. It is all we can do." Then
before I could think what to reply, he regained
mastery of himself and announced it was almost
time for meeting and he would summon the others. I
felt he wished to tell me something more but could
not part with the words. We have had so many
unconsummated moments – but today we were
almost father and daughter.

The mention of "sunset" may be a reference to the occasion, described by
Emily in a letter to Austin in 1851, on which Edward rang the church bell
to call the town's attention to a brilliant aurora borealis.

An April day adheres –
As it were gem
Embroidered on the edge
Of Nature's hem –

And sparkles as she moves –
A subtil glow –
Reflecting memory
Of ones we knew

[97]

Thursday, March 19

I began the day "sweetly" by making a batch of
chocolate caramels to send to Mr. Carter. He is now
at home recovering from surgery and may be cheered
by an unexpected gift. Perhaps he cant enjoy them
yet – but they will keep for his appetite's return. I
was obliged to sample one or two – to assure myself
the mix was right!

For a body or soul distempered – a taste of sugar
can be reviving. Chocolate and cream are pleasing to

the tongue. Words heated to a boil likewise make a
smooth confection!

The March 12 *Express* noted that S. C. Carter, town clerk and treasurer, had undergone an operation for fissure of the bowels and removal of tumors. He was reported to be doing well.

This candy was a specialty of Emily's. She sometimes sent it to friends as a New Year's gift—and obviously on other occasions as well.

 [98]

Monday, March 23

A week ago I heard a robin sing – and when I went
outside I almost touched Spring. Streams of melting
snow rushed everywhere – and the air – less frigid
– bespoke surrender.

But Nature loves betrayal! Winter never planned
so pliant a departure and – admitting the hoax –
regathered it's forces. March cant be trusted. On
Friday the snows returned – the worst storm of the
season – lasting till Saturday. Now the world is
white again, covering our hopes. But this death we
<u>know</u> is transient – We only suspect it of the other.

It was reported in the March 26 issue of the *Express* that the most severe snowstorm of the season had begun the previous Friday and continued through part of Saturday.

March is a cruel mistress
Enticing us with balms
That flood our wintered hearts with hope –
Then disappear in whims.

Lulled from our caution
By her passionate embrace –
We feel a new pain when – again –
She turns her icy face.

[99]

Sunday, March 29

Again I use the morning of the Lord for writing
while the others seek his presence in the pews.
Perhaps my soul is lost because I do not bow before
him there as well. Or perhaps God – like the World
– merely smiles at me. We two have been at odds –

but when the sun of His creation streams across the desk and lights my own I am filled with a strange presumption whose boldness frightens me. Can He have chosen me though I never gave myself to Him? Then I feel as if "grace is poured into my mouth" and I write what is too sacred to speak. It is not the grace of doctrines – but a gift unsought. Acceptance is both duty and salvation.

The quotation is from Psalm 45:2.

There is a brief – uncommon Fire
That singes – suddenly – and where
The coalless ember sears –
We feel a burnished difference
Transporting us past time and Sense
To unimagined spheres.

Who fears the ardor of the Blaze
Confines himself to arctic Days –
A slave to cooler Task –

Who would not flinch from that rare Flame
Accepts an Agony sublime –
Reward is in the Risk.

[100]

Friday, April 3

An April day adheres – and this one fixes me
forever to a golden memory! Judge Lord stopped
briefly and unannounced. He had not thought he
would have the opportunity to visit. Father was not
at home – but we served ably as his agents in
civility. Welcome is no chore for a guest so frequent
and beloved.

He stayed but an hour. Mother was called to a
neighbor and begged forgiveness for the interruption.
Vinnie then remembered chores in town – and her
eyes smiled as they touched mine.

Once more we two were alone. At first I could not
trust to speech – but he was braver. A single word
became a flood – and left us breathless – as on that
first afternoon.

He treasures Mind more than it's earthly vessel.
O friend who sees the heart's remotest longing –
drink deeply from this humble cup – and find how
sweet the wine within. Never shall you thirst – nor
ever be satisfied.

He has banished thoughts of those who had no
time to taste. But – like them – he is intangible –
and Sympathy the only glass we share.

That single hour was divinest draught – intoxi-
cation for Eternity.

The passionate tone of this entry presages that of the later letter drafts written to Lord. In one of these, placed by Johnson in 1878, Emily wrote, in language suggesting that the courtship had been one of some duration, "Dont you know you are happiest while I withhold and not confer – dont you know that 'No' is the wildest word we consign to Language?

"You do, for you know all things – [top of page cut off] . . . to lie so near your longing – to touch it as I passed, for I am but a restive sleeper and often should journey from your Arms through the happy night, but you will lift me back, wont you, for only there I ask to be – I say, if I felt the longing nearer – than in our dear past, perhaps I could not resist to bless it, but must, because it would be right.

"The 'Stile' is God's – My Sweet One – for your great sake – not mine – I will not let you cross – but it is all your's, and when it is right I will lift the Bars, and lay you in the Moss – You showed me the word."

Although this excerpt reflects an intense longing, some of the other passages suggest an ambivalence about where her love for Lord might lead (present also in No. 69). For while she herself not so subtly suggested marriage in one of the later letters ("Emily 'Jumbo'! Sweetest name, but I know a sweeter – Emily Jumbo Lord. Have I your approval?"), elsewhere she seemed less eager for surrender: "It is Anguish I long conceal from you to let you leave me, hungry, but you ask the divine Crust and that would doom the Bread." As early as 1878 she said, "Oh, my too beloved, save me from the idolatry which would crush us both – ."

The conflict between surrender to love and preservation of artistic freedom is a thread running through the diary and through the whole of Emily Dickinson's life. Perhaps ultimately she feared that the "idolatry" of love would somehow undermine her power as a poet.

For whatever reason, if Judge Lord did in fact propose marriage, Emily never assented. During the years of their open courtship she was much occupied in taking care of her invalid mother and, in addition to her deeper concerns, may have felt that this duty precluded other possibilities.

Mrs. Dickinson died in November of 1882. In March 1884 Judge Lord died of a stroke. Though in poor health the last two years of his life, he, like Edward Dickinson, kept up his regimen of hard work until the end. Emily later said of him, "Calvary and May wrestled in his Nature."

When Emily herself died in 1886, Vinnie put flowers in her coffin "to take to Judge Lord."

The Food to me denied –
Yet has my tongue – untried –
The art to taste
Were that defaulted Bread –
Unbroken – never fed –
Bestowed at last

Then would I savor bliss –
Though I be hungerless
Until I dine
In holy Luxury –
To eat – to sip – with thee
Enchanted wine.

 [101]

Wednesday, April 8

This evening I have been copying poems into the
little volumes. Some – from this book – I will
include if the Melody adheres when I return to
them. I wrote this one today while there were visitors
below. Pastor Jenkins and his wife stopped by this

afternoon to discuss a church matter with Father. I
made my appearance and bestowed what pleasantries
were required – then left them with my black cake
and good wishes and fled upstairs. My retreats – I
think – are by now almost expected!

Alone in my room I see the collection grow.
To string the verses together is a shaping endeavor.
We must make our own patterns as God wont
reveal His. One year I copied hundreds over – many
from girlhood – just to feel Creation's heft!

Now I place them in their "Alabaster Chamber."
Faith tells us that man's similar repose is tem-
porary – Immortality his destination. Shall these –
Life's Representatives – travel there as well?
Today the World takes gold for dross – but time
enhances value.

"Little volumes" presumably refers to the packets (Mabel Todd called
them "fascicles") of about eighteen to twenty poems each, which Emily
began assembling about 1858. Each packet consists of four, five, or six
sheets of letter paper folded and looped together with thread through the
spine. According to Johnson's dating by the handwriting, fascicles were
assembled for all poems between 1858 and 1865, and three were put

together later, in 1866, 1871, and 1872. This entry indicates that Emily was copying either new or previously existing poems into packets in 1868 as well. If packets exist for the poems in this diary, they have not yet been found.

The packet poems are all fair copies or semifinal drafts in ink and account for two-thirds of her entire creative output. The rest of the poems are worksheet drafts in pencil, written on whatever paper was handy— envelopes, recipes, wrapping paper, etc.

The largest number of poems in the handwriting of any one year is that from 1862. Packets from that year contain 366 poems—most of them final texts—and it was long assumed that these represented the production of one extraordinarily creative year. Emily's confession in the second paragraph that one year she had "copied hundreds over" shows this supposition to be false; if handwriting analyses are accurate, 1862 is the only year to which "hundreds" of poems can be assigned.

In the last paragraph she refers to her poem number 216, "Safe in their Alabaster Chambers," of which there are two versions (1859 and 1861).

(216)

Safe in their Alabaster Chambers –
Untouched by Morning
And untouched by Noon –
Sleep the meek members of the Resurrection –
Rafter of satin,
And Roof of stone.

Light laughs the breeze
In her Castle above them –
Babbles the Bee in a stolid Ear,

Pipe the Sweet Birds in ignorant cadence –
Ah, what sagacity perished here!

[1859]

Safe in their Alabaster Chambers –
Untouched by Morning –
And untouched by Noon –
Lie the meek members of the Resurrection –
Rafter of Satin – and Roof of Stone!

Grand go the Years – in the Crescent – above them –
Worlds scoop their Arcs –
And Firmaments – row –
Diadems – drop – and Doges – surrender –
Soundless as dots – on a Disc of Snow –

[1861]

Death renders no decision –
Appearing at the Bar –
But sends us back for Judgment
Where our Cause was heard before –

Remanded to our Father,
Who made the first Decree
Fixing the changeless dockets
That order Destiny –

We wait our Patrimony –
The heavenly Estate –
That passes to the Future –
Life's only Surrogate.

 [102]

Sunday, April 12

This morning there were bluebirds in the garden.
The snow is mostly melted – and now they busily
explore the life it hid. At last – I can breathe more
deeply – hearing again the light tread of spring. I
went for a stroll around the grounds. The sun so

modified the chill that I forgot it's sting and my
cape was sufficient warmth. Nature spoke clearly, as
if she knew "This is the day the Lord hath made."

The folks returned from church, relating that
Mr. Jenkins' sermon was, in Father's words, "not up
to his usual" and that the Kellogg girl was baptized.
The ceremony and the child quite impressed Mother,
who chattered unrestrainedly at dinner about both.

Father said nothing and merely turned his
attention to carving the fowl, but as Mother's
description progressed, I saw him glance at Vinnie
and me with an expression I could not define. It has
unsettled my mind up to this hour. Was it a
transient shadow of regret that we have no offspring
to share with the baptismal font? I always thought
he wished us never to leave his hearth. We have had
few suitors – but those he never discouraged –
though on occasion his disapproval was plain! He
has no high regard for the <u>mind</u> of woman – which
leaves a place of respect only for the role decreed by
Nature. Perhaps after all these years – seeing
Opportunity foreclosed – he worries that he played
a part in the foreclosure.

But I may interpret him unfairly – attributing to him the doubts of others. I know how the World regards the Dickinson daughters – for our lives never followed it's Prescription. Vinnie is acquainted with the town – and it with her! If Society knows less of me and therefore makes it's own mold, I cannot take notice. My Life is an exquisite secret – which not even Vinnie shares.

Much from me has been withheld – but that conferred surpasses men's imaginings. Privation remunerates. Christ taught us how to sacrifice the present for the Future.

I will not bear offspring of the flesh – but know a holy Consolation. God has fitted me for Conception of a different sort. My children are of the Mind – my Gestation perpetual – my Ecstasy of the soul. I welcome the joyous travail that separates the poem from it's creator – with no Midwife but the divine! Now let ages take the measure of Fecundity – and the Future judge whether this choice – if choice – was right. These things I would explain to Father – if I could – and ask him to be patient for the Harvest.

The quotation in the first paragraph is from Psalm 118:24.

Edward Dickinson died in 1874. Emily died in 1886 of Bright's disease, a kidney disorder. The first edition of *Poems* by Emily Dickinson was published in 1890. Thus neither father nor daughter witnessed the harvest.

About the Author

Photo: Back-in-a-Flash, Austin, Texas

Jamie Fuller holds degrees in English, Russian, and law and has spent most of her professional life as an editor with various book publishers. A licensed but nonpracticing attorney, she currently works as a legal editor in Austin, Texas.

By avocation Fuller is a poet, translator, and amateur scholar. Her translations of Russian verse have been published in *Russian Literature Triquarterly, The Ardis Anthology of Recent Russian Literature, The Ardis Anthology of Russian Romanticism,* and *Russian Literature of the 1920s. The Diary of Emily Dickinson,* her first book-length work, is the product of sudden inspiration, countless hours of enthralling research, and many joyful months of spiritual coexistence with the real Emily.

Design: Robin Price

Art direction: Sharon Smith

Illustrations: Marlene McLoughlin

Editing: Thomas Christensen, David Peattie,

Kirsten Janene-Nelson

Copyediting: Alice H. Klein

Production coordination: Zipporah W. Collins

Composition: The Bieler Press

Printing and binding: R. R. Donnelley and Sons